The Vanderhoof Conspiracy

(Based on a true event)

_____

Tammy Walls

The Vanderhoof Conspiracy

Copyright © 2018 by Tammy Walls

Supreme Court Ruling quoted at the end of this novel is a matter of Public Record.

ISBN 9781731536440

Printed in the United States of America

Dedication

This book is dedicated to those whose lives were taken too soon, and for whom the real cause of their deaths remains a mystery to this day.

Know this - Dead men do tell tales– Even a hundred and thirty -five years later!

Acknowledgments and Special Thanks

Special thanks to my son, Jeremiah Ryan, author of Monsters Walk Among Us, whom through his inspiration, tireless cover designs, and suggestions helped me to complete this lifelong desire.

Special thanks also to my husband – the inspiration for the character Robert in this book, and a victim of my endless hours of typing and talking through scenarios in this book.And finally, a special acknowledgment to Ella Vinton, a life long since passed away, and the author of the diaries to which I found the notation about the Vanderhoof trial that started me on this journey, so many years ago. Little did she ever imagine that a simple line that she penned in January of 1884, would evolve into a book and bring to life the trial of her neighbor, Elizabeth Vanderhoof.

Table of Contents

Preface

The Vanderhoof Conspiracy is a fictional story based upon an actual court trial that took place in 1884. It was pure coincidence that I stumbled upon this trial while going through some diaries that I had acquired at an antique store many years ago. Interestingly enough, that trial is used as a basis for modern-day court decisions.

While the trial did occur and several factual details are sprinkled throughout the book, the remaining portions of this book and all conversations are fictional and the imagination of the author. The names used, related to the events that occurred at that time, are names of actual people long deceased. Any events in this book that reference modern-day use fictitious names, and all events of modern-day are completely fictional, and the imagination of the author.

Please note that there are two stories which interweave throughout the book. One is modern-day, and one is in the past.

Chapter 1
The Mystery Begins

June 17, 2018, Michigan

With an air of frustration about him, the heavy set police officer entered the interrogation room. Hastily he pulled out a chair and sat across the table from Lynn. His expanding belly that was barely being held in by his white shirt pushed tightly against the rim of the table in front of him. He placed his large chubby hand on the table and tapped his fingers with impatience as beads of sweat ran down the side of his face. It was mid-June, and the air conditioner in the police station had been broken since last year.

"So, do you want to tell me what is going on, Miss?"

Lynn pushed her brown hair back from her eyes. "I already told the other officer. What is the matter with you people? Why are you not taking me seriously? I told you guys that I have someone following me and peering in my windows at night, and you sit there and act like I am inconveniencing you! Whatever happened to we serve and protect? Emphasis on the protect!" she asked indignantly.

"Look, lady, don't get smart-mouthed with me! If you have an issue, you're going to need to start from the beginning and give me exact details and descriptions of your stalker. When did it start, etcetera, okay?"

Just then the metal door opened, and in walked another man. He was not in a police uniform but instead sported a crisp white shirt and blue tie. His hair was reddish-brown, and he was slightly balding. His glasses reflected the lights in the room but did not hide his light brown eyes that were fixated on her like two lasers. The Police Officer that had been with her turned when he heard the door open, and after seeing who it was got up from the chair and exited the room without so much as a word between the two of them. The tall good looking detective walked over to the table but did not sit. He stood carefully looking at her, studying her, and finally, he stated, "I am detective Webster. I understand you are filing a report because you claim to have a stalker."

"I don't claim to have one. I have one!" she blurted. "You know what, I don't need this cynicism! You are the third person to talk with me. I have been here for two hours! If you don't want to help me, then maybe I can get someone else to help me; like an attorney. And maybe he will be interested to know how the police would not help me and take me seriously." She stood up to leave.

"I don't think you quite understand the situation, Miss."

"I think I understand it quite well! I think it is you who doesn't understand! I have come here for help, and none of you seem to care or be willing to help. Now, if you will excuse me," she said, moving her thin frame around the side of the table.

"I'm sorry, but I cannot allow you to leave," the detective said, giving a quick nod to the other man.

"What do you mean when you say that you can't allow me to leave?"

Almost on cue, the door opened, and the fat man that was in the room before entered and was accompanied by another short-stocky man with hairy arms. "This way, Miss," the fat man said.

"What's going on here?" She stood her ground momentarily and looked at the two men and then over at the detective who motioned with a nod of his head to the other two men. And without another word, they each grabbed her by the arm.

26 years earlier: 1992 Rochester, Indiana

"How much do you want for these diaries?" Lynn asked the clerk at the antique store.

"Well, I'm not sure," the young girl managed to say while simultaneously popping a bubble with the gum she had been chewing. "My mother runs the store, and she is not here today. I could probably reach her by phone. Do you want to wait?"

"Yes, I'll wait." Lynn placed the seven diaries down on the counter. The diaries looked more like old-time store ledger books to her, but she was eager to get them. She fidgeted momentarily while the clerk dialed the phone. She glanced at the books again and noticed that there was writing on a yellow sticky note on top of the diaries outer cover. Two of them said "mother's diary," while the other five stated "daughter's diaries." They dated from eighteen hundred sixty-three to nineteen hundred twenty-four. After thumbing through a few pages, she glanced around the store. It was an unorganized mess, but just the kind of antique store that she loved. Treasures were waiting here, and she believed that she had found some. The old pole barn building that served as this antique store was behind an old house off the main road. The house was run down, and there was a bunch of clutter in the front yard. Old glass insulators from early electric lines sat perched atop the fence that bordered the front yard. The sign that had pointed the way from the main road was the only indication that this place was back here. Lynn heard the clerk talking and turned back towards her.

"Hi, Mom, there is some lady here who found some diaries in the back room and wants to know how much they are. ...Um, hold on, I'll ask her...Which spot did you find them in?"

"They were in the side room over there. I found them in a box under the bottom shelf."

The girl repeated, "She says they were in a box under the bottom shelf in the side room. ...Um, there are seven of them. ...Okay,... yes, okay, thanks, Mom." After hanging up the phone, she turned towards Lynn and said, "She said she hasn't finished reading them all, but she will sell them and take thirty-five dollars for the set. She said they belonged to a mother and a daughter where the mother started writing in eighteen hundred sixty-one until her death, and the daughter picked up in eighteen hundred eighty-one and wrote the rest."

"Okay, I'll take them!" Lynn eagerly paid the clerk and headed towards the door. She wanted to get out of the store quickly, lest the mother called back and decide she didn't want to sell the diaries. She was so excited because she had always been intrigued by the time period that these diaries covered and couldn't wait to get home to read them.

Bursting through the door to her home, she found her husband and said, "Look what I found at Four Oaks Antiques - diaries! I can't believe it! Seventy plus years of who knows

10

what!" She plopped her recent acquisition down on the table and picked up the youngest of her three children. Turning back towards her husband, she continued, "Why would anyone get rid of their family diaries?"

"Wow, honey," he said jokingly, "You just found story writing material for the next ten years!" Lynn was a writer and always looking for another storyline.

January 2014 - 22 years later

"Now remember, you're not to get up and walk around on that foot, and if you must get up, use the knee walker!" Lynn's husband, Robert, emphatically commanded. She just had foot surgery and was ordered to stay off her feet for a week.

"Well, what am I supposed to do for a week, especially while you are away at work?"

"I don't know. Maybe read a good book or something. Wait! I know! How about reading those diaries that we keep moving around? You know, the ones that you never finished?"

"They were boring. They're just one line of daily activities of so and so did this and so and so did that. They are really boring! The only cool things are some old photos and miscellaneous receipts that are in them."

"Well, if they are so boring, let's get rid of them. Why are we keeping them?"

"No, I will not get rid of them! They're over one hundred and fifty-years-old! Bring them to me. I'll give them one more chance."

She began reading the diaries without much interest. Some of the entries were in pencil, and the years had caused them to fade, making reading difficult. She was reading December eighteen hundred eighty-three when she came upon the text that read, 'Mr. Vanderhoof died today.' She said out loud, "Someone is always dying! These poor people!" She read a few more entries when one jumped off the page. It read, 'Charles went to the Vanderhoof trial today.'

"Wait. What?" She sat up and flipped back to December to re-read, 'Mr. Vanderhoof died today.' Eagerly her fingers followed the entries until she again came to the words, 'Charles went to the Vanderhoof trial today.' "What trial?" She continued to read on eagerly. But there was no other mention that month of the trial. Quickly, she pulled out the laptop that Robert had left next to her, and she began a search for any references to the Vanderhoof trial. Several entries popped up that referenced the trial and verdict, but the reference was just noted there for other modern court cases. She was beside herself with curiosity. What happened? She just had to know. Breaking her promise to stay off her feet, she hobbled over to the cabinet to retrieve a few of the other diaries. Opening them, she shook them until some photos, and a few other papers fell out. She picked up one of the papers. It was a letter from an attorney which simply stated, "Mr. Charles Vinton, your presence is requested at the courthouse to testify in the trial of Elizabeth Vanderhoof, Monday, at nine o'clock in the morning. "

June 18, 2018. Four years later and one day after Lynn's disappearance

"Yes, Sir, how can I help you?" the young dark-haired officer asked Robert as he entered the police station. Robert's thin frame and narrow lips were trembling. He removed his ball cap, revealing his thinning brown hair.

"I don't ... He swallowed hard. "I don't know where my wife is. She didn't come home from work, and I can't reach her by phone."

"How long has it been?" the officer questioned.

"Just today. She should have been home hours ago. It's not like her. I saw her this morning before I left for work, and when she didn't come home, I tried to call her. There was no answer. I called several times and left several messages. Then I contacted her work. She works in a nursing home. One of the nurses put me in touch with her boss, and she said my wife texted this morning to say she wasn't coming in. But that's not like her either. She would have told me if she had the day off. She never hides anything from me. Her boss stated that she had texted my wife back to ask if she was sick, but my wife never responded."

"Sir, have you checked the hospitals to see if there has been an accident or anything?"

"Yes, of course, and there is nothing. Officer, you don't understand. She told me a couple of times that she thought she saw someone looking in the window at the house. I didn't think much of it because we have a dog. He hears everything. If there were somebody out there, the dog would have been going crazy."

"Sir, is it possible...."

Robert interrupted. "Today is her birthday. She was excited that we were going out to supper with her children. She doesn't get to see them as much as she likes, and she was very excited. Something is wrong. This isn't like her." He choked back tears.

"I understand your concern, Mr. ....."

"Willis, Robert Willis."

The officer's eyes widened just slightly. Robert now had his full attention. The officer looked at him from his head down to his feet, in a scanning motion, as if he was sizing up an opponent. He reached over and hit a button on his phone. "I understand your concern, Mr. Willis, but technically, we cannot open a missing person's report until twenty-four hours have passed."

"Twenty-four hours? She could be in dead in twenty-four hours! You expect me to wait twenty-four hours?"

"Sir, I know this sounds bad, but it happens a lot. Is it possible, I mean..." He stumbled over the next words. "Have you considered that she may have just left you?"

Robert stared blankly at the officer. Then in an increasingly elevated tone, he said, "My wife didn't leave me. We have a great marriage. I am telling you my wife had complained about a stalker and now she has disappeared. Don't you think that means anything? Have you ignored that information and just jumped to the 'maybe she left you routine?"

The police officer bristled. A stern look came across his face indicating that he didn't appreciate the tone that Robert had just used.

"I'm sorry," Robert apologized. "I didn't mean to offend you. I'm just really worried. Can you please help me? Please!"

"Is there a problem here?" A voice from behind Robert startled him, causing him to jump. He turned around to find a tall reddish-brown haired man standing there. "I'm detective Webster. Can I help you?"

"Yes, Sir. I told this officer that my wife is missing. She didn't go to work, and I can't get hold of her. I have a feeling she's in danger."

"Why is that, Mr...."

"Willis, Robert Willis." The Detective looked up at the man behind the desk, and the two men locked eyes for a moment. "She kept saying that someone was stalking her, but I didn't believe her, not because I thought she was lying, but because I never saw him."

"Isn't that the same thing?" the detective asked.

"What?"

"If you didn't believe her, then you must have thought she was lying."

"I'm not sure what you're getting at. All I know is that she would say a man was standing in the road staring at the house, or that she was getting strange calls at work. One time she said there was a car following her."

"And why did she think someone would be following her?"

"I don't know. She thought it had something to do with the diaries that she had."

"Diaries? Now, I'm not following you. What do you mean?"

"It sounds crazy, I know. But she found these diaries, years ago, and she had surgery this year and had nothing to do, so she started reading them. She said she found out about a murder case or something, and then she started researching it by going to the courthouse and asking at the library. Then she noticed people were following her. I don't know, but is there a way for you to trace her phone or something?"

"Murder case? Sir, how about you come with me?" Robert nervously followed the detective passed several desks. One female officer, who had been eavesdropping on the conversation, watched him intently as he passed by her desk. Her gaze made him even more uneasy than he already was. The Detective led him to a side room but did not close the door. "Have a seat, Mr. Willis. Now, start from the beginning. What is all this talk about a murder case?"

"Well, I don't know," he said, placing his baseball cap upon the table in front of him. "You see, my wife found these diaries years ago. I wasn't married to her at the time. She had never fully read them. I think she just got busy with life and three kids. Anyhow, a few years back, she had foot surgery, and I suggested that she read the diaries to give her something to do. That's when it all started."

"When what started?"

"When she started saying something about a murder that happened years ago. I thought she said eighteen hundred eighty-three and how some property was stolen and something about a horse being taken, and that there was some type of a cover-up. Anyhow, she started obsessing about finding out what had happened and started going to the courthouse and the library. It was shortly after that when she said someone began following her. I'm telling you, something has happened to her. Please, Sir, can you help me?"

16

The Detective sat back and stared at Robert. "Yes. Yes, I can help you. We can fill out a missing person report. Did your wife have any documents that tied into this quote-unquote murder?"

"I don't know," he hung his head. "I don't know."

"Would you mind if I came by your home tomorrow to take a look around?"

"If you think it would help to find her."

"Yes, I think it would help. Now, if you would fill out this form, and give it to the officer out there on your way out. Oh, and we will need a photo of her. And don't worry. We will do all we can, Mr. Willis. I'm certain your wife is okay. Most of the time, these things tend to work themselves out."

Robert filled out the form and slowly walked up to the desk where the blonde-haired girl, who had stared at him earlier, sat. Gingerly, he reached out and handed the form to her. She stared at him and then glanced over her shoulder back towards the interrogation room, but the Detective was no longer there.

"Is there anything else that I need to do?" he asked. "How long will it take until you notify the other counties? When will you call me?"

"Sir, we will do everything we can," she said quickly. "Now, is this statement here correct?" She pointed to a line on the police report in front of her where there was a small note that she had written and placed on the top of it. It only said one word, "danger." Robert crinkled his brow and slowly looked up and met her eyes. She motioned with her eyes towards the back of the room where the Detective had been.

Slowly, he nodded and said, "Yes, that is my statement," and turned to leave.

"We will be in touch, Sir," she called after him. "Don't worry. We will find your wife!"

He left the station but sat in his car outside for several minutes. What did that note mean? What should he do? Who could he turn to? He was lost in thought when a loud tapping on his window startled him, and he jumped. It was another police officer, one he had not met. This man was older with a bit of gray hair and had a rough texture to his skin.

"Something I can help you with?"

Robert rolled down the window. "No, I was just leaving. I just filled out a report inside."

"Alright, but you can't sit here. You're going to have to move along."

He started his vehicle still not knowing what to do. The drive wasn't long, but the closer he got to home the sadder he became. He dreaded walking into the empty house. He reminisced about the first time that he had met Lynn and how it was love at first sight. Tears began to stream down his cheeks. Turning down his road, he began the small descent down the hill towards the lake. His home was on a dead-end private drive along the lakefront. There were only four other homes on the same side of the lake as his.

He stopped prematurely at the end of the hill and turned off his lights and parked the vehicle in front of the lake. It looked so beautiful tonight, he thought, with the moon gleaming across the surface of the water. He took a long drag from his vaporizer while thinking about his wife and the note that the police officer had written. The word danger kept filling his thoughts. After taking another drag, he looked down at the vaporizer. Lynn hated that thing. She had hated him smoking real cigarettes, too. He finally quit those but seemed to be unable to give up vaping. How he wished he had a real cigarette right now. He made himself a promise that if she were okay and returned home safely, he would quit vaping. He would do anything to have his wife back. Why did it have to come to this to do something that she wanted? He was mad at himself for smoking. He was mad at himself for not believing her about the stalker. Why? Why didn't he believe her?

He looked up towards the moon and prayed. "God, I know you are listening. Please, God, I am begging you. Please let Lynn be okay. Please help them find her." Then, after wiping away a few tears, he again looked at the moon. He remembered how two weeks earlier she had gone away for a week of training for work, and when they were on the phone she told him to look out the window up at the moon, and then she romanticized how they were both looking at the moon together even though they were apart. He took another long drag and was about to start the Jeep when something caught the corner of his eye. His dog, Napoleon, a six-year-old brown and white pit bull terrier came trotting along the lake. "What the hell, how did you get out?" he muttered. The dog was never allowed outside without a leash because there was no fence in the yard. If he was out, Lynn or Robert was always with him. Glancing over his shoulder towards his house, he was just about to open the vehicle door when another motion caught his attention. Only this time, it was from inside the house. A light flashed from the side room. It wasn't the main light but a flashlight. Fear gripped him all of a sudden as he remembered the note from the police officer. He looked around slowly and then as quiet as possible opened the Jeep door and motioned to the dog. Obediently, Napoleon bounded into the vehicle. Robert climbed out and then gently closed the door so that it made only a click to secure the dog's safety. He sneaked towards the window of his home and was starting to peer inside when he heard the slow rumbling of a vehicle's tires coming down the hill. He glanced in that direction, but there were no headlights. Quickly he couched, ran, and hid behind the bush at the corner of the house.

Since there were only four homes along the road, He was familiar with who came and went. Only two of the four owners stayed year-round and the others usually only came on the holiday weekends. The car that drove slowly was not familiar to him, and it seemed to pause when it passed his vehicle at the end of the road. He could make out only one figure inside, but couldn't tell if it was a male or a female. As the vehicle passed his home and pulled into the neighbor's drive to turn around, he quickly climbed the half-cement wall between his home and his neighbor's home. He ran passed it and across the back of the next home. Once he was around the side of that house, he quickly crawled towards the lake and gently lowered himself down. As quiet as he could, he swam behind his neighbor's boat lift for cover. From that location, he could still see his house and the mysterious car.

As the vehicle reached the front of his home, it again slowed. Napoleon could now be heard barking from inside the Jeep. The driver of the vehicle heard the dog, and the car stopped. Suddenly, a spotlight was turned on and shone towards the Jeep. The dog was on all fours barking loudly. The spotlight scanned the front of the house and then the yard and then around the area. Robert stayed low in the water. He still could not make out the occupant of the vehicle, but he was really scared now.

He was scared for Lynn and where she could be. He was scared for himself and scared for the dog. The vehicle's spotlight went out, and the car pulled away. Robert waited for what seemed to be an eternity, but in reality, was about twenty minutes. Then, he slowly climbed up the back of his neighbor's boat lift and into the boat. He would stay there until the morning.

The early morning lake activity woke Robert. He peeked out carefully and then felt safe to climb down. Arriving at his vehicle, he found that the dog was still there and very happy to see him. He pulled the Jeep into his driveway just a short distance away. As he approached the house, he noticed that the back door to was ajar. Carefully pushing open the door, he let the dog go inside first. If someone were still there, they would be in for a nasty surprise. Napoleon didn't take kindly to people he didn't know. After a few moments, when the dog did not bark, he felt safe to enter. He looked around. Everything seemed to be in place. Everything, that was, except Lynn's closet. The clothes had been rustled through, and some were scattered hastily on the floor. All the suitcases that were usually nicely stacked in the back of the closet were pulled out, and he couldn't tell if anything was missing. As he continued to look, he noticed that the small fire safe was gone. That was something Lynn had always kept in the back of her closet. She told him that she kept her important papers in there. Someone had found the safe. Yes, someone had been in his home, but who and what were they looking for?

Napoleon came in the room as if he, too, were looking for Lynn. And as Robert looked at the dog, it suddenly occurred to him -Napoleon was outside last night. He wouldn't have just left the house if someone were inside. It would have taken some doing. He had a loud and fierce bark and would have drawn attention, especially since the homes on the lake were close together. He would not have obeyed a stranger unless it wasn't a stranger, Robert reasoned. Unless it was someone that the dog knew. Either it was a familiar face, and he left the house willingly, or the door had been left open for a long time so that the dog would leave on his own. Either way, whoever was in his house would have needed the dog out of the way. Suddenly Robert remembered that his neighbor, Scott, had a video surveillance system. He darted from his home across the drive and knocked feverishly on Scott's back door.

Scott was an older man, tanned from his life of retirement but very kind and very smart. He had been at the lake almost as long as Robert had, and the two had a great bond and frequently helped each other out with whatever project that one of them was doing.

"Hey, Robert, how are you?" Scott said, answering the urgent rapping at his door.

"Scott, can I come in? Please, it's urgent!"

A quizzical look came over Scott's face, but he pushed the door open, allowing Robert to step inside. "What's up?"

"Are your outdoor cameras still working?"

"Yes, why?"

"I know you are going to think I'm crazy, but can I see the videos from yesterday and last night?"

"Yeah,….". Scott said slowly, "What's going on?"

Robert broke into the short version of what had happened and ended his tale with, "...and so I'm trying to figure out who was in my house and what kind of car that was last night? Can you help me out?"

"Oh, my God! Robert, I am so sorry- about Lynn, that is. You know I will be here and if there is anything at all that you need...." He stopped short of finishing his sentence. "Robert, have you called the police since last night?"

"No."

"No? Are you crazy! You need to call them. You don't have any idea who that was or what they wanted. Robert, you need to call them."

"Yes, yes, I will. But right now, I need to do a little digging on my own."

"Alright, I'll be right back. Let me get my I-Pad. We can put the images up on the television." He hurried to get his I-pad while Robert nervously stood, staring out the window towards the lake. It was busy today. Boats were buzzing by pulling skiers or kids on tubes. He looked over at his boat and choked up a bit. Lynn loved the Supra. They had just purchased it last year after getting rid of the old Mark Twain that he had for many years. He thought about how much they enjoyed taking boat rides at night or just jumping off of it in the middle of the lake. He was lost in thought when Scott returned and positioned himself at the table in the great room where Robert was. Within a few minutes, the video recordings from the previous night were playing. Due to the proximity of their homes, the cameras were able to pick up activity on Robert's property too. The two men scanned the footage carefully.

"There! There..." Robert pointed. "Back up. See that? Who is by the back door?"

"I can probably enlarge it," Scott said. "Um....it looks like Lynn. Yeah; it is Lynn."

Robert stared at the frozen image. "This is from yesterday? What time was that?"

"Two ten in the afternoon."

"Two ten? That's about an hour and a half before I got home. That doesn't make any sense. I texted her all day."

Scott backed up the image. "Look, there at the corner of the garage." There was a movement where the cameras caught only a glimpse. Together they studied it, rewound it and watched it again. It was definitely a person. They turned their attention to Lynn. Her position at the back door would have left her completely exposed to the stranger, yet she did not act as if she was concerned.

"Wait a minute. Let me see what the other camera picked up." He clicked through some keys on his I-pad and pulled up images from the camera towards the front corner of the house that angled backward on his driveway. "There!" The video showed Lynn and the stranger having a brief conversation. At one point, she looked towards Scott's house and motioned with her hand for the other person to stay back. Then she entered the house briefly and left just as quickly, bounding out the back door and up the stairway on the back hill.

Scott sat back. "I'm really sorry, Robert."

"Sorry? Sorry for what?"

"Well, it looks like…., You know. You know what it looks like."

Robert got up and paced. "No,….no,…., she would never….". He walked towards the door.

"Robert, wait a minute. Please, hear me out. You have to call the police. You don't know if those people will be back."

"I will, Scott. I will." Robert walked out the door and back towards his house. Once inside, he went back to Lynn's closet and started to look through it. He had no idea what he was looking for, but he was looking. What did she come in the house for and what did she take out? Or did she take something out? Or did she put something inside? He was digging through her things when there was a knock at the back door. Napoleon jumped and barked, causing Robert to jump. Cautiously, he made his way to the back door and peeked out of the kitchen window. It was the blonde-haired officer that he had met the night before; only she was not in uniform. He walked over to the side window and glanced at his driveway, but there was no vehicle there.

Robert opened the door, and the dog took his place next to him. Robert just looked at her and didn't say anything.

"Mr. Willis, may I come inside? Please, we need to talk."

"How did you get here? Where is your vehicle?"

"I parked it at the top of the hill near the grove of trees and came down the back stairs. I did not want to draw attention to myself.

"And why is that?"

"Mr. Willis, may I please come inside?"

He opened the door, and she hurried inside past him. Napoleon turned and followed her and was busy sniffing her legs. She seemed uncomfortable with the dog so close. Normally, Robert would have called the dog back if he was bothering a guest, but this time, he didn't. He wanted her to be uncomfortable. He also left the door open, so the glass screen was visible, and he stood relatively close to it.

"Do you have any news about my wife?"

"No, but I have to talk to you. May we sit down?"

"Something told me that you didn't come here to talk about my wife. So why exactly are you here, Miss...?"

She didn't answer his prompting for her name. Instead, she sat on the nearby sofa and repeated, "Please, may we talk?"

He was still leery of her. After last night, he would have been leery of his sister. Now, he wasn't sure who this person was and if he could trust her. Finally, whistling to the dog, Napoleon left the woman, and he and Robert sat across the room.

"What's this all about?"

"Mr. Willis, I am not who you think I am."

"Really," he said sarcastically. "How would you know who I think you might be?"

"Look, it's a long story, but...."

"I think I have plenty of time," he interrupted.

"I'm an undercover FBI agent. My name is Maggie Martin."

"Do you have any identification?"

The short blonde reached in her coat pocket and pulled out a badge and an ID. He looked at it briefly, and then blurted, "What the hell is going on here?"

"Robert," she paused, "May I call you Robert?"

"Yes."

"Robert, I was put on this case about four weeks ago."

"What case?"

"The Vanderhoof case."

"Excuse me? The Vanderhoof case? What are you talking about? What does this have to do with me?"

"Your wife was digging into information about a trial -the Vanderhoof trial, and well, your wife found out that there was an

26

illegal plan many years ago to take property away from a woman named Elizabeth Vanderhoof. That was the land that she had inherited from her first husband and land that was very valuable. Apparently, your wife started asking a lot of questions, and people started to sit up and take notice. You see, Mr. Willis, some have something to lose if it is discovered that the property was stolen."

He didn't say anything but got up and took a drag off of his vaporizer and looked out over the lake. He could hear Detective Martin still talking in the background, but he was focused out on the lake. It was odd, he thought, the floating wooden turtle raft that he had placed in the water on the right side of the pier had been moved over to the left, and the paddle boat was now on the right side when it had previously been on the left. His eyes scanned the lake. Everything else seemed to be where he remembered it. Or maybe he didn't remember it at all. Maybe he was wrong about the turtle raft, but surely the paddle boat was on the wrong side of the pier. He never put it on the left.

"Mr. Willis," the Detective interrupted, "are you listening to me?"

He snapped out of his stare. "Oh, I'm sorry. I was lost in thought."

"Yes, I am sure you are. But as I said, I will need to see any documents that she may have had."

"Um, I'm sorry, Detective. We will need to do this another time. I just can't do this now."

"You don't understand, Robert. If you don't show me what she had, then I'm not going to be able to find her. I can look around if you don't mind." Her urgent tone took him by surprise.

"I do mind, and we will need to do this another time." He walked over to the door and opened it. Napoleon stood also.

Detective Martin looked at him and then over at the dog and said, "Of course. I will come back, maybe tomorrow."

He closed and locked the door behind her. Everything in him felt that something was wrong, no, that everything was wrong. He didn't know what, but he knew one thing -he had to find out what was going on and from the event the previous night with the intruder, he knew he could trust nobody around here, except Scott. But even then, he wasn't willing to risk Lynn's life on him either.

He walked over to the coffee maker and started a pot of coffee. While he waited for the carafe to fill, he picked up his cell phone and began to look through the texts that Lynn had sent him over the past week. The dog was now at his feet, whining, so he put him on a leash and went out in the back yard. He sat on the stairs that led up to the second story of his garage and flipped through the texts, while Napoleon sniffed at the grass below. One of them stopped him. It was a short string of texts between him and Lynn. It read:

(Robert) *Hi Baby, how are things today at work? What's for lunch?*

(Lynn) *Hi yourself, things are okay. How about you?*

(Robert) *Good, nothing interesting.*

(Lynn) *Hey, I wanted to let you know that I finally planted the Chrysanthemum flowers that your Dad bought us.*

(Robert) *Great! What do you want to do tonight?*

(Lynn) *Don't know. Probably finish gardening. I LOVE the Chrysanthemums.*

(Robert) *Okay, well I have to run. Love you.*

He stared at the texts. What the heck? he thought. My father didn't give us Chrysanthemums. He gave us a peony bush. Curious, he Robert the leash and walked towards the front of the house. He stared at the landscaping near the front deck and looked at the pink Chrysanthemums that Lynn planted just recently. They were beautiful. He had given her them to her for their anniversary. He furrowed his brow. Why did she say my father gave those to us? Plopping down on the stairs of the deck, he stared at the flowers for a moment reminiscing about the night that she came home from work and he had the flowers and a card sitting on the table waiting for her. She was so excited. She loved flowers.

Suddenly, his thoughts stopped and turned back towards the string of texts. Then like a bolt of lightning, he grabbed the dog's leash and jumped up. He walked around the back of the house. Pretending to walk the dog around the yard, he casually strolled over to the white peony bush. It looked as if it needed some water, which was odd because none of the other plants were drooping like that one was. He also noticed that the red mulch around it seemed a bit dirtier than the other sections of mulch nearby. He stared at the plant and remembered what she had said, 'I planted the Chrysanthemums that your father gave us.' He again looked around and pretended to walk casually towards the house. Once inside, he closed all the blinds and began rummaging through everything. Where were the papers that Lynn had been working on? He had seen her numerous times with legal pads and documents that she had sent off for or made copies of. And where were the diaries? He couldn't find them anywhere. He went through her drawers and turned her closet

29

inside out. Nothing. Then he found the box where she kept her only gun; a Baretta Tomcat. He took it out and loaded it, then turned towards Napoleon and said, "I think this is a good idea, don't you?" The dog looked at him and wagged his tail. "Come On, Napoleon, let's do some gardening."

Robert put on some work gloves and headed out to the garage. Grabbing a wheelbarrow and a shovel, he went over to the peony bush and began to dig. Just then, Scott came out of his garage. Seeing Robert digging, he called, "Anything I can help with?"

"No, just trying to keep busy. It looks like this bush would do better in another location."

Scott acknowledged the fact and waved as if to say, "Understood." Robert turned his attention back to the task at hand and plunged the spade into the ground once more, and this time, he heard an unusual crinkle noise. He tried not to make any unusual motions so as not to draw attention to himself just in case someone was watching. With the next plunge of the shovel, he went into the soil deeper than the last time and scooped up a large lump of soil under the small plant and put the entire thing into the wheelbarrow. He could vaguely see a plastic bag peeking out from the bottom of the soil mound. Trying to be sure that nobody else saw it, he quickly scooped another shovel full of dirt and threw it over the top of the mound already in the wheelbarrow. Spinning around, he wheeled everything back into the garage as Napoleon trotted happily behind him. As soon as the door closed, he grabbed the plastic bag that was in the soil and pulled out the contents. They were all the notes that were in Lynn's handwriting that he had been looking for. He shoved them down his pants, headed back into the house and grabbed the keys to his Jeep. Whistling for the dog, Napoleon bounded from behind and eagerly followed Robert to his vehicle.

As he drove down the country roads from the lake, he was careful to watch and see that he was not followed. He turned down several obscure roads and zig-zagged until he knew for sure that he was alone, and then he made his way to the expressway and headed an hour and a half away towards the home of his lifelong friend, Doug.

It was getting towards sundown when he arrived in Cedar Lake, Indiana, the sleepy little town where he had grown up. After the initial shock of finding Robert on his doorstep unannounced, and Robert telling him what had been happening, the two men sat together in the family room, away from the other members of Doug's family. Robert took out the papers and started reading them out loud.

Chapter 2
The Death of William

November 30, 1883, Galien Michigan, Berrien County

"Lizzy, Lizzy!" William Vanderhoof shouted from his bed as the sun was setting on that cold evening in November. His long, lanky body thrashed about as he writhed in pain. He was unable to say much but continually called out for his wife as he threw the covers on and off in a restless sort of way. His bedclothes stuck to his body from the immense sweat that had been generated by his fever. It was the third time that night that the sheets and his bedclothes were changed. At one point in the night, he had soaked the bed so thoroughly that he had to be moved to the other bed in the room.

"I'm here, Willie. I'm here," Elizabeth Vanderhoof, his wife of nine years, said as she took her place in the chair next to her husband's bed. Her small thin frame sunk into the chair from exhaustion. She had been up and down the stairs multiple times over the past week as William's health continued to decline. Slowly, she pushed back her long brown hair that had fallen into a disheveled mess from her once tightly pulled bun. Her hair did not cover her crystal blue eyes that she had; eyes so clear and sharp that they looked like glass. William continued to call for her as if he couldn't see her, until his father, who was standing nearby, spoke up, "What will you have, William? What will you have?" But William didn't acknowledge his father's answer and continued to call out

Jennie Lind, the couple's middle daughter, stood off in the corner chewing on her nails and watching the scene unfold before her. She was never allowed in their bedroom, and this was the first occasion to which she found herself there just waiting and watching. Her older sister, Lydia Jane, joined her and pulled Jennie's fingers from her mouth. "Stop it! You know mother doesn't like you to chew on your fingers!" But Jennie was scared. She didn't know what was wrong with her Papa, and she had never seen him act in this manner. And Jennie wasn't alone. Others were watching him, too.

"William, what it is you will have?" Thomas asked again when William kept calling out for Elizabeth. Thomas Vanderhoof was the patriarch of the Vanderhoof family. He was tall and thin, like William, but slightly deeper of complexion. His graying beard protruded past his chin, and his ears were somewhat large. He was the son of David Vanderhoof, one of the counties first settlers. The Vanderhoof family was powerful and wealthy, having been the first family to build a home on one of the Indian Reservations in Berrien County. Thomas stood next to Tryphena, his second wife. He had married her after William's mother died several years back. Tryphena was a beautiful woman with long blonde hair. She was short and petite and much younger than Thomas. Tryphena was William's age, and they had been taught together by the same schoolmaster. Her marriage had been arranged through her father, who wanted to purchase some land from Thomas near Christiana Creek but didn't have the money to do so. As a compromise, he had traded his daughter for the land.

William continued to ignore both Elizabeth and his father when they responded to his incessant calling. He continued to thrash about and would occasionally shout out, "My God, help me! It's so hot in here! I cannot breathe!" But it wasn't hot. It was late November, and Lizzy had opened the windows in the small upper bedroom because he had been calling out that it was hot. The cool evening breeze blew steadily in, so much that Thomas walked over and closed the window after a while, and the others in the room had put on their winter coats.

William's twin sister, Sarah, was also there. She, too, was tall, but not lanky. She was curvy, and a redhead, like her mother, Mary, had been. She had not left her brother's bedside since this illness had worsened. She continually doted on him, putting a damp cloth on his head or his chest in an attempt to give him some relief. Sarah was close to William, but she did not fancy Lizzy and had disliked her from the beginning. She never told anyone why she disliked her so much, but Thomas always speculated that Sarah didn't think Lizzy was good enough for William. She always thought that William had married her out of pity and desperation. She didn't know how close to the truth she actually was.

Also in the room were Ella and Charles Vinton who were their neighbors to the south. Ella and Charles were members of two other families that had been early settlers. They had come to help Lizzy care for her children and do the chores that William was no longer able to do. Ella was a very petite and plain woman, but kind as the day was long. She loved children and would often gather them together after the church meeting and handout whatever treat she had made for them. Ella was also a writer and kept meticulous diaries. After her mother died in eighteen hundred eighty-one, she had taken her mother's diaries and picked up writing where she had left off. Every day, there was another entry, and every month at the top of the diary page, was a Bible verse. This event, too, of William Vanderhoof and his illness, would make the diaries.

Charles, on the other hand, was a hardworking rugged man, who never had a lot to say, but was also loved by the neighbors. He was always around to lend a helping hand and the first to offer anything that would be of help to someone in need. He worked tirelessly helping to shape the county, build the schools, and plan the roads.

And there were two other ladies, Hattie and Avella Long, who had come to bring a meal for Elizabeth and her children. Neither had ever married, so they lived together and cared for one another.

Finally, tired of listening to William cry out, Tryphena blurted, "Elizabeth, I am going to give him a dose of his tonic. Maybe it will help? I cannot stand to see him in such pain." She walked over and caressed his wet hair. "Don't worry, Willie, I'm going to get your tonic. The Doctor is on his way. Can you hear me, Willie? I'll be right back."

Elizabeth didn't break her glance of William's face, but replied, "It's downstairs in the cupboard, on the right side." Slowly she stood as if to help, but then collapsed back down into the chair. "Tryphena, please mix two tablespoons of the tonic with water."

Tryphena hurried down the stairs as if she were on a hurried mission. Her shoes could be heard clunking about the wooden floor downstairs and then back up the stairs. "Here, Willy, darling. Take this. It will help." She positioned herself next to the bed and cradled his head in her arms. His thrashing about almost spilled the tonic on several tries. Elizabeth grew tired of watching the scene in front of her and decided to get out of the way and went to stand over by the window. She gave out a loud sigh causing Sarah to glance up at her and wonder why she wasn't helping Tryphena. But Lizzy was fixated, staring outside, almost in a daze.

William was being difficult, shaking his head back and forth. "No! No!" He kept saying. Finally, Thomas intervened helping to hold his head still while Tryphena put the medication in his mouth. "Come now, William. Take your medicine."

"Yes, Willy, this will help with the pain," Tryphena emphasized. In frustration, she added, "I wish Dr. Mann would get here. Where is that hired hand of yours, Lizzy? The doctor's residence isn't that far away, for heaven's sake!" She was, of course, referring to John Chapman, a very handsome blonde-haired, blue-eyed man with a toned physique to match. John had come to help on the Vanderhoof farm after learning that William had taken ill. He was the one chosen to go into the cold winter night to fetch the doctor. It seemed an eternity had gone by since he had left.

"Here they are!" Elizabeth said as she stepped back from the window and walked quickly towards the bedroom door and down the stairs.

The entry door opened, forcing the cold air inside. "How is he, Lizzy?" the doctor asked while taking off his coat and handing it to her.

"Not well, Sir. I fear this may be the end. Please, go up and see if there is anything you can do for his comfort."

"Have you given him the tonic recently?"

"No, Sir, I haven't."

The doctor hurried up the narrow stairway towards the upstairs bedroom that he had become so familiar with over the last several months.

Looking over her shoulder quickly to make sure the doctor was gone, Elizabeth turned to John Chapman. "This is taking so long!" she said in a soft worried tone of voice.

"It will be over soon, Lizzy. He will be out of his suffering soon." John walked forward and placed his hand upon her arm and rubbed it, trying to console her.

"Yes, I know, but it didn't take this long with Nathan. This is so difficult to watch."

"Just remember the goal, Lizzy Stay focused on the goal."

"And what would that goal be, Mr. Chapman?" Sarah said appearing, from what seemed to be, out of nowhere, but in reality, she had come down the stairs right after the doctor, and the noise from the shoes had been mistakenly believed to be from the doctor.

Both John and Elizabeth looked startled. "My apologies. I seemed to have interrupted a very interesting conversation. I am overtaken with curiosity, though, Mr. Chapman. What goal do you think my dear sister- in- law should focus on?" She stressed the word 'dear' very sarcastically.

"Sarah! How dare you take liberties within my home!" Elizabeth snapped. "Do not be so emboldened to involve yourself in a conversation that does not involve you! Now, if you will excuse me, I must go check on my husband!" She spun around and climbed up the stairs quickly, leaving John and Sarah alone.

Sarah sauntered over closer to John and threw back her hair from her shoulder in a flirty type of manner. "So, Mr. Chapman, you were saying about a goal?"

"Since you were so bold as to interject yourself into our conversation, I will indulge you. I was referring to heaven and the goal of being in the arms of our Lord. That's the goal she needs to be focused on in such a time as this. I was encouraging her not to focus on the pain and suffering, because that will soon be over."

"Really, Mr. Chapman, you? A church-going man? Come now, don't you find it curious that my dear sister-in-law had married my brother, who himself was the hired hand for her first husband that died, and now she seems to be on quite familiar terms with you, the new hired hand?"

John stepped forward, almost close enough to kiss her and said in a whispered tone, "The only thing I find curious is that you don't see what a good woman your sister-in-law is. She has born children to your brother and doted on him during this illness. I have watched her sit up all night and read to him to calm him from the panic that overtakes him when he cannot breathe, and then watch her go out and do the chores without getting any sleep for herself. But you wouldn't see that because you are jealous that she is such a good person and you are a wicked-minded spinster!"

"Well! I never!" she started to say.

"I'll bet you haven't!" he said and walked past her, bumping her in the shoulder on his way up the stairs.

He found Lizzy standing at the foot of the bed. William sat up and called out for her, reaching for her, one last time, "Lizzy!" And then he collapsed backward. The doctor listened to his heart while everyone in the room remained silent, almost frozen. Then he looked up at her, "I'm sorry, Mrs. Vanderhoof, and you too, Thomas. He's gone."

Elizabeth gasped loudly and said, "Oh, John, don't leave me!" And then she fainted. John Chapman, who had taken a position closely behind her, caught her as she collapsed backward. Thomas Vanderhoof, who had been standing with his head hanging downward, looked up quizzically at Elizabeth as she called out John's name. John scooped her up and quickly carried her over to the other bed in the room. Tryphena and Ella both rushed to her side. Ella quickly loosened the ties on the front of Lizzy's dress while Tryphena attempted to fan her to get her some air. "Get a cool cloth," the doctor ordered, and John bolted from the room and returned with a rag and quickly placed it on her chest, to the shock of the other ladies.

Thomas walked over and grabbed John by the arm. "Do not attempt to take liberties with my daughter -in- law, Mr. Chapman."

"I meant no disrespect, Sir. I can assure you. I was only trying to help. I'm truly sorry. It was instinct. I have medical training from the war. If I overstepped my boundaries, again, I meant no disrespect, Sir." John stood up, handed the wet cloth to Ella, and made his way towards the bedroom door. On his way out, he passed Sarah, who had been standing in the back of the room. She smirked as he passed her.

Elizabeth wearily sat up. Seeing the fussing ladies next to her, she asked, "What is happening?"

"Sit up slowly, dear," Ella urged her. "You fainted."

"Oh,"...she paused, "Oh, no! William!" She pushed aside Tryphena to see William's lifeless body laying there. "Oh, Willie! Willie, why did you have to go?" She buried her head on his chest and cried. Ella gathered the children and escorted them out of the room.

"Come, Tryphena," Thomas reached for her arm. "We should give Lizzy a few moments." Tryphena hesitated. She didn't want to leave, and her body language suggested it. Thomas tugged again at her arm, which she pulled away momentarily and leaned over to kissed William on the head.

"God speed, William, dear, dear William." She began crying and left the room with Thomas in tow.

After a few moments, Lizzy stood up, straightened her dress, and walked over towards the window. Again she peered out, staring into the darkness.

"Well, that was short-lived," a voice from behind startled her. It was Sarah. She hadn't left the room. She was still standing in the back of the room.

Elizabeth spun around in surprise. "Sarah! You nearly scared me to death!"

"I'll bet I did. Your tears dried up pretty quickly."

"Sarah, this is not the time for your bitterness."

"Bitterness? Do you think I have bitterness? Let me tell you what I have. I have disdain, Lizzy, for you and your lies!"

"I am unsure as to what you are referring Sarah, but do not suppose for one instance that I am the weak ill-equipped widow that cannot handle the likes of you! And also do not suppose that I will allow you to wipe your boots upon me! You have

41

crossed the line twice now in my home, and I ask you to leave this instant!"

"Oh come now, Lizzy. You don't think I was the only one that heard your little slip of the lip, do you?"   Then she mockingly continued, "Oh John, do not leave me!" She walked closer to Lizzy. "Didn't you mean to use Willie's name in your little fainting episode?"

"I never said any such thing!"

"Oh, but you did, dear sister-in-law. How very convenient that John happens to be around to pick up where William left off. Or has he done that already?"

"Sarah! I will not stand here and allow you to speak to me in such a vile manner! I am glad William will never know how wicked his sister behaved towards his wife!" She spoke in a slightly raised tone of voice, in the event others were listening. Then she turned to storm out of the room and down the stairs, but just before opening the door, she stopped, turned, and walked up close to Sarah and said in an eerie whispered voice, "You would be well advised to stay away from me!"

The burial for William was at the Galien Cemetery underneath a large sycamore tree. It seemed as if the entire community was in attendance that day, and after all, why wouldn't they be? The Vanderhoof family was one of the oldest in the community, and Thomas often spoke at the meeting house when the Pastor was not going to be there.

Donned in black garb, Elizabeth stood graveside next to the large monolith that had been carted there and set the day before. The stone simply said, 'William Vanderhoof, eighteen hundred forty-eight to eighteen hundred eighty-three, aged thirty-five years. That was it. William's life was condensed into seven words. The wind howled and whipped at Lizzy's bonnet, but she stood firm and made her girls stand with her. As the Pastor prayed, Lizzy looked up. Across the grave from her stood Sarah. She was glaring at Elizabeth and made certain Lizzy saw her whisper in Tryphena's ear who then also looked up and stared momentarily.

As the men began shoveling the soil over the casket, Lizzy began to walk away and back towards the waiting buggy. The same buggy that John Chapman had driven for her. He had stood in the background while the services were going on. After his run-in with Thomas back at the house, he did not want to draw attention to himself or Lizzy. Sarah was also walking back to her father's buggy, when Captain Sterns, the local druggist, tugged at her arm and motioned for her to slow down.

"Sir?" she replied.

"Sarah, it's urgent that we speak."

"And what might this be in regards to that you feel the need to interfere in my family's mourning?"

"Your brother – it's in regards to William. It's urgent, Sarah. Please, come by the shop as soon as you are able."

She looked at him momentarily, and he repeated the word 'urgent.'

"Okay, then I shall call upon you tomorrow." She turned to leave but then quickly called out to Elizabeth. "Lizzy! Lizzy! May I speak with you a moment?"

Lizzy turned to her girls and motioned for them to go to the buggy and wait for her. "Yes, of course, Sarah." She approached her half expecting a cordial conversation when Sarah moved in close so that she could not be overheard by the others

"If you think for one moment that you will get any of my brother's prize horses or his money, you are sadly mistaken. I will see to that."

A smirk came over Lizzy's face. "Oh, Sarah, dear confused Sarah. It would seem that the law is not in your favor." She moved as if she was going to leave but then turned to say one final thought, "You know, Sarah; I was thinking the other day about snakes. Do you know what is so scary about a snake, Sarah? You never hear them coming and then they strike when you least expect it! A word of caution. Don't play with snakes, Sarah." She walked away but made sure that Sarah saw John help her up onto the buggy.

December 3, 1883 – One day later

Sarah Vanderhoof entered through the squeaky front door of the druggist's store. It was another windy day, and the door eagerly slammed to a close behind her. Captain Sterns, the druggist, looked up. Seeing who it was, he quickly took off his glasses and tucked them into his black vest pocket. In an attempt to make himself more presentable, he ran his hand over his dark, slightly greasy hair and rushed towards her.

"I am so glad you came. Please, Miss Vanderhoof, come with me." He motioned towards the back room.

"Mr. Sterns, that is in no way appropriate. After all, what if someone were to come into the shop and see us in the back room together. It would not be easy to defend."

"Yes, yes, of course. My apologies, Miss. Please, wait here.".

He disappeared into the back room, and Sarah could hear him rustling about items and not being too quiet about whatever it was he was doing. Finally, he came out with a small stack of accounting journal books. He pulled out his glasses, and after hastily placing them on his face in a sort of crooked manner, he categorized the books until he came to one that was marked eighteen hundred seventy-six. He opened it and quickly ran his fingers down each entry. Finally finding the one he was looking for, he turned the book around on the countertop so that Sarah could see. "Look. Look here."

She looked down and read the entry. It was dated March first, eighteen hundred seventy-six and stated, .' Sold to Elizabeth Salisbury, one-ounce arsenic.'

"Dear Captain, I am afraid I do not understand why you are showing this to me."

"Nathan... Nathan Salisbury, her first husband...," the Captain was speaking hurriedly but hushed at the same time. "Miss Vanderhoof, and I mean Elizabeth – well she was Salisbury at the time, she purchased this right before Nathan died."

"I am afraid I still am not following you."

"Maybe this will help." He fumbled through the books once again and came to the one marked with the year eighteen hundred eight-three. "Look," he said as he quickly pointed to another entry. It was dated September thirteenth, eighteen hundred eighty-three. It read: 'Sold to Elizabeth Vanderhoof...' Sarah stopped as she read the next three words – ." She looked up as the Captain began muttering, "It all just came to me, the day I heard that your brother had died. I remembered Elizabeth coming in here looking for something to get rid of rats. She

45

stated that she had rats about the house and in the barn, and the doctor had been out to the house and told her to get poison for the rats. I remember finding it odd that while she said she was looking for something that she specifically mentioned needing arsenic. I didn't think about it again until Mr. Vanderhoof died."

"Captain, what are you saying?"

"After Mr. Vanderhoof died, it just seemed too familiar to me. I couldn't remember the exact year that Mr. Salisbury died, so I took a trip to the cemetery to look at his headstone. Once I realized it was eighteen hundred seventy-six, I hurried back and went through my journals until I came across the one with the entry from eighteen hundred seventy-six. Don't you find it — how shall I say — unusual? " Then in a more subtle tone of voice, he added, "Ma'am, I am trained in the apothecary. I am familiar with the effects, both good and bad, with my mixtures."

She took a deep breath and looked down at both journals again. Her eyes darted back and forth between the two. "Mr. Sterns would there be a way to test for certain mixtures, even after a person had passed?"

"Yes, Ma'am. The sooner, the better before the body would continue to decompose."

She swallowed hard. "May I take these books? I promise to return them to you at a later date."

"Yes, of course."

She scooped up the books and quickly walked out the door, through the snow, and across the road to the Sheriff's office.

Chapter 3
The Sheriff Gets Involved

Sarah Vanderhoof paced back and forth upon the wooden floor inside the jailhouse. Her boots echoed with each step as she became more and more impatient waiting for Sheriff Clarke to return from whatever had taken him away that morning. The only comfort that she had at the moment was that the jailhouse was warm, compliments of the wood stove in the corner, but oddly, the jail had a coldness to it. There was only one cell inside, and it was currently empty. The Sheriff's desk had a few items upon it and a large, dirty mug that looked as if it held yesterday's coffee. Across the room was a sloppily made cot where the Sheriff or Deputy slept at times when they had a prisoner to watch.

Finally, after what seemed to be an eternity, the door opened, and the Sheriff entered. He was a tall, burly man, well built for his occupation. Seeing Sarah startled him slightly, he removed his hat, "Ma'am?"

Without taking any time to inform the Sheriff as to the reason for her recent visit, she blurted, "Sheriff, I would like my brother's body disinterred."

The Sheriff got a quizzical look on his face, and before he could say anything to her request, she said, "Forgive me for my

47

manners. Please, sit down, Sheriff. You and I have a great deal to discuss."

He walked over towards the large wooden desk and picked up his coffee mug. In a half-hazard manner, he dumped the contents into the nearby plant and proceeded to refill the mug with the black coffee that had been sitting in a nearby pot. Finally, he found his chair and plopped down. He reached into his pocket to pull out a cigar. "Alright, Sarah. What's this all about?"

"Please refrain, Sheriff," she motioned towards the cigar. "I cannot tolerate the smell of those things." With a disgusted look on his face, he placed the cigar back into his pocket.

She continued, "I believe my brother's death was no accident. I believe that Elizabeth Vanderhoof may have murdered my brother."

"Murdered? Come now, Sarah, that is a very strong accusation."

"Maybe so, but I believe it to be true."

"Miss, it is well known that you do not get along with Mrs. Vanderhoof. So tell me why it is that I should believe what you are saying?"

"Sheriff, please do not insult me! This has absolutely nothing to do with whether Lizzy and I were good friends. You see, Sheriff, it all started right after she and Willie got married. I need not add, that being twins, my brother and I were always very close. And I began to notice things. Many things. Especially after he met that Elizabeth, that is when he began to change."

"Miss Vanderhoof, all men change when they get a woman in their life. But what kind of changes are you speaking of specifically?"

48

"No, Sheriff, no. You misunderstand. I know you are relatively new to these parts, but she was married before to Nathan Salisbury. He had served with my brother in the war, and Nathan had been crippled by a bullet in his lower spine. And as we were led to believe, the infection that it caused spread through his body, and he became very sickly."

"What does this have to do with your brother?"

"Everything. Lizzy was weary of caring for him. I overheard her tell Ella Vinton that very thing one day after Sunday meeting. Lizzy was in a hurry to get back to their farm because one of their horses was ready to give birth, and she asked Ella's husband, Charles, to help get Nathan into the buggy. While he was doing that, I overheard her tell Ella that she had grown very weary of caring for Nathan. She stated it was like having another child."

"Are you telling me that Elizabeth, who can't be over one hundred pounds, would lift her husband into a buggy each meeting day?"

"No, that is not what I am saying. His father lived with them, and her father was on the farm right next to them. But that is neither here nor there. It matters not to me how they got him to the meeting. What matters is that she made it known that she needed help on the farm. And that is how she and my brother became acquainted. I did not know, until after they married, that Nathan and William served together in the war."

"Go on with your story."

"Soon after my brother began working on the Salisbury farm, Nathan's father's health began to decline, rapidly. At least that is what William said. And then old Mr. Salisbury passed away suddenly leaving everything to Nathan. If you don't know it,

Sheriff, the Salisbury family was well to do and owned extensive property in Ohio as well as here in Michigan. And it was shortly after the death of Mr. Salisbury that Nathan began to get worse and worse. And eventually, he died as well."

"What was his cause of death?"

"I will get to that, Sheriff, but it is important for you to know that she filed for his estate in March of eighteen hundred seventy-six and married William two months later. I dare to say; she was not a grieving widow! And, I also heard that there was talk back then regarding Nathan's sudden death. Don't you think if people were talking about it that they must have found it odd?"

"People talk, Miss Vanderhoof. Sometimes they talk about things that are none of their business."

"Sheriff if you are implying that my brother's death is none of my business?"

"I am not implying that. I am simply saying that people talk and sometimes they don't know what they are talking about. Please, go on."

"It was about four years after they had been married when I overheard Elizabeth telling Ella Vinton that my brother had been harsh with her. He wanted her to sell the property back in Ohio, and he wanted her to sell the northern part of her current land her in Galien. That was the land that was left to her after Nathan died."

"Why was that?"

"So that my father could open a mill. You know, Sheriff, that property has the river running through it, and the Salisbury family bought it quickly when they heard my father wanted the land."

50

"So why then did he want her to sell the property in Ohio?"

"So that he could use the money to purchase more land here. And she told Ella that day that she and my brother had a sharp disagreement about it."

"So you were eavesdropping on their conversation? How do you know you heard the entire story?"

"Oh, I heard it and more. But she didn't know that I heard it. Just like she didn't know that I overheard her and Mr. Chapman, the hired hand, talking the night William died."

The Sheriff sat up. "What did you hear the night William died?"

Sarah smirked and brushed a piece of her reddish-blond lock from her eyes. I see you are now interested in...,what did you call it, Sheriff,....my story?"

"Miss Vanderhoof, If you have something that you think I should know, please go on. If not, I am very busy."

Sarah looked around the room. "I would hardly say that you are very busy. And I will go on with my story. The night William died, I overheard Lizzy and John Chapman talking secretly downstairs right after the doctor had arrived. She was saying that it didn't take this long with Nathan and he said, for her to focus on the goal. When I made my presence known, they gave me an excuse for what they were saying, and she scolded me for listening."

"Did they say anything else?"

"No, but you know, Sheriff, it was shortly after I had overheard her conversation with Ella Vinton when my brother began to have stomach issues. I remember talking with him, and he said, Sarah, it is bewildering. I simply can't seem to enjoy a meal any longer. Soon after I eat, I have tremendous stomach pain; then I feel as if I can't breathe and am going to faint. Those were his exact words Sheriff. And furthermore, the doctor wasn't looking at his stomach. That doctor was only prescribing things for his heart and telling Willie all the while that it was his heart. It wasn't his heart that he began complaining about. It was his stomach."

"What is your point?"

"My point is that I don't believe my brother died of a weak heart, Sheriff. Nor do I believe that Mr. Salisbury died of natural causes. I think that both of their deaths were hastened by Elizabeth Vanderhoof."

"Sarah, are you proposing to me that Elizabeth murdered both of her husbands?"

"That is what I am proposing. And furthermore, I demand that you look into it and have my brother's body examined."

"Miss Vanderhoof, what would be the motive for Elizabeth to do such a thing?"

"Money, Sheriff. Plain and simple. She gained control of the Salisbury fortune by getting Nathan Salisbury and his father out of the way. And she stands to get my brother's money as well. It is no secret to anyone in Berrien County that we are well to do."

"I am going to need more than your accusation to justify having your brother's body dug from the grave."

Sarah unlatched her coat and reached inside to retrieve the two journals. She placed them onto the desk in front of the Sheriff. "Maybe these will convince you?" She flipped the journals open and found the entries that Captain Sterns had shown to her earlier.

"Where did you get these?" the Sheriff stated after looking at them.

"From Captain Sterns."

"The druggist? When did he give this to you?"

"Earlier today. He accosted me yesterday, after the burial, when the others were walking back towards the buggies. He asked to speak to me privately and asked if I would come to the store. I left there a short while ago."

Sheriff Clarke looked down at the entry again from September thirteenth, eighteen hundred eighty-three. The words jumped off the page as if they were screaming at him. 'Sold to Elizabeth Vanderhoof one ounce – arsenic.'

Chapter 4
Robert and Doug

Back in Vandalia, Michigan, modern-day

"I don't understand," Doug questioned Robert. "What does any of that have to do with Lynn? It's just a bunch of notes about some family from the eighteen hundreds and some pictures and stuff."

Robert looked up and shook his head from side to side. Sitting back, he took a swallow of his beer. "I don't know. What I can tell you is that she found these diaries, years ago, before I ever met her. And she found out about some guy who died. I think his name was William Vanderhock or something like that. Anyhow, it turns out that whoever wrote the diaries made a note that there was a trial about his death. That is what she started digging into. She took a week off of work last month and spent days going to the courthouse and digging through old documents. That is when she said she was followed."

"Come on," Doug said. "It isn't like this is some big-city crime ring she is busting. The guy died over one hundred and thirty-five years ago. What could it possibly have to do with her missing?"

"So you think it could be something else?" Robert asked.

"It could be. Maybe she stumbled on something else while she was researching this stuff."

Robert nodded. "Well, if she did, she didn't mention it to me. Then again, I only half-listened to her sometimes. She tends to ramble." He choked up a bit. "I wish I would have listened to her."

"So where did you get those papers?" Doug asked.

"I was going through my phone looking at the last text messages we sent to each other, and something in one of them caught me a bit by surprise. She was talking about flowers that my father gave us, but he never gave us flowers. He gave us a bush."

Doug leaned back and folded his arms across his chest. "I'm not following you."

"Lynn liked to do puzzles and watch mysteries. As a matter of fact, we recently went to some 'Who Done It' supper theater type of thing. And I realized she was trying to tell me something in her text when she mentioned the flowers."

"So this is some kind of a game?"

"No, it's not a game. She always sent coded text messages if she was trying to give me a hint about stuff -like our anniversary. Kind of crazy isn't it?"

Doug looked bewildered and rubbed his chin. "Yeah, crazy." He took in a deep breath, sat forward and said, "Well maybe she left you some other hints. Let's go through those texts again."

Robert grabbed his phone from his vest pocket and scrolled back through the texts.

"Wait, let me get some paper," Doug said, jumping to his feet. When he returned, he said, "Okay go through them, all of them, even the ones you won't think matter. Maybe we can find something."

Robert began reading each text as Doug scribbled keywords onto the note pad. Robert came to a text that said:

(Lynn) - Hey baby, just saw the cutest thing. Baby turtles were trying to get onto the turtle raft and as hard as they tried, and they couldn't.

Doug looked up with curiosity. "What's a turtle raft?"

"It's just a floating piece of wood anchored by a block and it....". He stopped. His mind quickly flashed back to when he was staring out the window earlier at his house.

"I don't remember seeing it when we were at your house for the birthday party."

"You probably did and didn't know it. It was the wooden platform about two by two that was in the shallow water."

"You mean that thing floating in front of your speedboat?"

"It was in front of the speedboat? Wasn't it on the other side? Are you sure?"

"Yes, positive. I remember seeing a piece of wood there because I remember your dog kept walking down the pier and staring at it. I remember wondering what he was doing."

"That would mean that she moved it before the party. That was brilliant. It would not have drawn any attention. It would have looked like she was moving it to the other side so she could set up the water volleyball net."

"What are you talking about, Dude?"

Robert didn't say anything.

"Come on, what gives?"

"It's a clue, Doug. Don't you see it?"

"What kind of a clue?"

"Well, she hid these papers beneath the bush. She wanted me to find them. That's why she left a note in the dog food bin.

What if she hid something beneath the turtle raft? I need to go back and take a look."

"Now wait a minute. You are starting to scare me. I think we should call the police. You have no idea what is going on or who was following her or what in the world they would be looking for. How do you know you aren't being followed? Oh, my God, Dude, how do you know that you didn't bring whoever here? I have kids!"

"I wasn't followed, Doug. I'm certain of it. I was careful. But now, thinking about that turtle raft, I do need to go. I have to check if there is anything else she wants me to find."

"I'm going to go with you. You don't know what you could be walking into. Wait a minute. Let me get my gun."

The two men headed back towards Vandalia, but Robert had been wrong. He was followed. He had always been followed.

There wasn't any other talking on the way back, but the reading and re-reading of texts to see if there was anything else that might give a clue as to what happened to his Lynn.

Arriving at Union Road, Robert slowly drove towards his home, being careful to look at the surroundings.

"Look," Doug said. "Is that the turtle raft-the thing in front of the speed boat?"

"Yes, but I didn't put it there. I never put it there."

"You must have."

"I'm telling you that I didn't. She moved it."

"Why would she do that?"

"It's something she knew that I would notice.; just like the bush and flower mix up. Only she and I would pay attention to where the turtle raft was, and she would know that I would see it out of place."

"I'm not following."

"I found the papers under a newly planted bush in the back yard. She told me in the text something only she and I knew about that bush, and then she left a note in the dog's food bin knowing I would find the clue. She was leading me to it. And just like that, it just came to me to look there."

"Come on, Dude. This is getting a bit weird."

"The question in my head is how did she move the raft? It's anchored with a cement block. It isn't that light. She had a lifting restriction from her last surgery. That wouldn't have been easy for her."

"So?"

"So, we wait until dark."

"Dude, you are creeping me out. I really think we need to call the police. And I definitely need to call my wife and let her know I will be late."

As the sun was setting, Robert made his way towards the boat. He and Doug were planning a late-night cruise – something Robert had done often. As the boat idled to a slow stop some distance from the shoreline, Robert sneaked over the side and down into the water. Having been on the swim team during high school, and living on the lake most of his life, he was quite the long-distance swimmer.

"Wait here and pretend to carry on some conversation as if I am with you. Remember, voices carry. I will be back in a bit."

"Alright, be careful. We should've thought of a signal."

Robert made his way quietly back towards his pier. As he approached, the neighbor's light suddenly came on, and Robert quickly skulked below his boat lift. Slowly the neighbor pulled out from his garage and down the road, and as the garage door closed, the lake once again grew dark. Robert quickly worked his way underneath the pier towards the turtle raft. Taking a large breath, he groped under the water until he found the large cinder block below. He felt around it and momentarily thought he had felt something odd but had to come up for air. Quietly breaking the surface of the water, he took another deep breath. He tried to stay as low as he could in the four and a half foot depth and feel with his foot. Yes, there was definitely something inside one of the pockets of the cinder block that anchored the turtle raft rope. He drew in a deep breath and went underneath the surface. Frantically, his hands groped the block. There was something tied there. It felt like a metal box. He couldn't get it undone and had to come up again. From what he could tell, the box was held in place by a knot on the right side. He would have to undo it. He stopped momentarily. In the distance, he could hear Doug talking. One last breath and he was under again. Pulling with his fingers as hard as he could, the knot suddenly broke loose. He held the box tight and slowly made his way back towards the boat.

"Dude you scared the crap out of me!" Doug whispered as Robert climbed up. "You know, bad things happen on lakes in the dark."

"Don't be crazy, but look, I knew it! She hid this. Let's get back and see what it is."

"Crazy?" he whispered back. "I'm not the one doing crazy things here."

"Wait." Robert stopped. "I can't just walk off the boat carrying this little metal box." He opened the box and grabbed the contents. "Here. You're dry. Stick this in your pants."

Obediently, Doug shoved the papers in his pants and untucked his shirt to cover himself. Robert quietly lowered the box into the water so that it didn't make a splash and let it go. They returned to the house, and Robert walked around inside the small cottage to make sure it was secure, and all the window shades were down. "Come on, let's go up here," he pointed to the ladder that led to the loft.

"Why up there?"

"In case someone can see through the blinds. They will never be able to see up here."

"Come on! Let's get out of here. You are totally freaking me out."

At that moment, Robert's phone buzzed, and Doug jumped. The number that came across the screen was not recognized. Without any hesitation, he answered the call. "Hello?" There was a lot of static on the other end of the line. He repeated, "Hello?" There was no response, but he could tell the line was connected, and he just listened for a few more seconds when he heard the other party hang up. Quickly hitting redial, the phone rang at the police station.

"Vandalia police, how may I help you?"

A bit surprised, he replied, "Hi, this is Robert Willis. Did you just try to call me?"

"No, Sir, I didn't just try to call you, but let me see if anyone else here did." Robert could hear the officer asking the others. He got back on the phone. "Sir, nobody here called you."

"Yes, someone did. My phone just rang, and it registered this number."

"Maybe someone dialed you by accident."

"Look, I am not trying to be difficult, but someone from there did try to call me. I can prove it to you. I can come there and show you that my phone registered a call from your office. Please, ask around again. I .....,". He stopped. Napoleon was growling, staring toward the back of the house.

"Sir? Are you still there? Sir?...," the officer at the other end waited.

But Robert was momentarily frozen. He heard a noise behind his house as if someone bumped into the large green garbage can underneath the back kitchen window. "I think someone is behind my house," he said in a low voice to the man at the other end of the phone.

"What do you mean, Sir?"

"I heard something behind my house, and my dog is growling."

"Would you like me to send an officer?"

"Yes, I think that would be a good idea."

"Are there any weapons in the home?"

"What? Why are you asking me that question?" He emphasized the word "me."

"It is for the safety of our officers. I will ask you again, are there any weapons inside the home?"

"Yes, I have a gun but . ." He stopped. He could hear the police officer whispering to someone on the other end. He couldn't make out what was being said, but he suddenly got a really bad feeling.

"You know what?" he lied. "It was just a raccoon. I turned on the backyard light, and he scurried away. You don't need to send an officer."

"I would feel better if we did. We will send our detective. He is over that way and in an unmarked vehicle."

"No, it's not necessary." Robert was motioning to Doug to come down the loft stairs. He quickly hung up and turned to tap the dog. Napoleon stopped growling and quieted down. Robert made his way over to the keys on his counter and quickly hit the alarm to his car. It began blaring. Within seconds, Scott's outdoor lights went on, and he was on his drive looking around.

Robert motioned for Doug and the dog to come, and quickly they entered the Jeep. Scott called after Robert to ask if everything was okay, but Robert just backed up and headed out.

"What the hell is going on, Dude?"

"I don't know. But someone wants to get something." He drove quickly up the hill and darted to the left. He would know soon if he was followed. The road curved quickly, and then there was a rarely traveled gravel road to his right. He quickly took that and then followed another route he knew that would get them out to the main road without being noticed.

"Dude, we can't do this anymore. You need to call the police," Doug said.

"Who do you think I just called? Don't you find it suspicious at all – the noise behind the house – the call from the police, but they deny it? I don't know what is going on, but I am not calling them."

"This isn't a movie, Man! This is real life! What about the FBI? Didn't you say that lady was an undercover FBI agent?"

"Yes, but I don't have her number with me. It's at the house."

"Do you remember her name? Can't we just call the FBI and ask for her? Robert, man, I don't want to scare you, but I am really scared. For some reason, we are in danger, and God only knows about Lynn?"

Robert choked up and looked blankly at Doug. "Sorry, Dude. That was insensitive of me. But I'm serious. We need to call the FBI."

Robert nodded and turned onto another road. He definitely was not being followed, or so he thought. Soon he and Doug got on the expressway and headed back towards Cedar Lake, Indiana. After they arrived, Doug grabbed his laptop and began furiously looking up information on how to contact the FBI. His blonde hair was disheveled, and he was looking a bit pale. "Here, try this number. If it's wrong, maybe they can direct you."

The phone on the other end rang, and Robert explained to the operator that he was attempting to get in touch with Detective Maggie Martin.

"I'm sorry sir, there is nobody here by that name."

"There has to be. Look I know you all are trying to protect one another in case someone who is crazy is looking for them, but I swear to you, I met her. She came to my home the other day, and she is the one working undercover at the Vandalia police department."

"Sir, I just told you that....."

"Please, ma'am. My wife is missing, and I am being followed."

She sighed heavily, "One moment, please." The phone went to some soft elevator-type music, and after a minute, a voice came on, but it was not the female voice he had spoken to earlier.

"This is Agent Harvey. May I help you?"

Robert went into detail on the events over the last few days. When he came to the end of the story, the Agent said, "Sir, I am going to need you to come to the bureau. Can you do that?"

"Where?"

"We are located in Indianapolis, Indiana."

"Yes. Yes, I can come. I will be there first thing in the morning."

He hung up the phone and turned to Doug. "They want me to go to the bureau in the morning. I think I will head that way tonight."

"Tonight? Umm...okay, let me tell Lisa. There is no way that I am leaving you alone. Safety in numbers, right?"

"What are you going to say to her? You can't just tell her we are going to the FBI."

"Don't worry about it. I'll handle it."

Robert shook his head in agreement and walked outside towards the Jeep. He was nervous and locked the doors. His eyes scanned the area around him. He felt as if he was being watched, although he couldn't see anyone. Doug returned a few moments later. Robert started the Jeep and headed towards Indianapolis while Doug pulled out the papers that had been in the metal box below the turtle raft and began reading them.

Chapter 5
Sheriff Clarke and the Prosecutor

Sheriff Clarke was pacing in front of the desk of the prosecuting attorney, James Kellogg. James was an older man of about sixty years of age. His well-manicured white shirt matched his mustache. He had lived in the community all his life and was a very well respected gentleman.

"Well?" Sheriff Clarke questioned. "What are your thoughts?"

Flipping through the journals, James slowly nodded his head. "I don't see that we have a choice. There is reasonable suspicion."

"Yes, I agree. But I think we need to tell Thomas first."

"That is something we absolutely should not do. If word gets out about what we are going to do, then it could derail this entire thing. No, we need to keep quiet about this. Can you get Jeremiah and Matthew here tomorrow, say about ten?"

"Yes, I can. And I know they will keep it quiet."

The next day was cold but sunny as Sheriff Clarke, James Kellogg, Matthew, and Jeremiah arrived at the Galien cemetery. Heavy snow had fallen for the last few days, and the grounds of the graveyard looked pristine, with no tracks, other than the occasional rabbit tracks. Buttoning his black trench coat, Sheriff Clarke pulled the collar up around his neck, climbed out of the buggy, and walked towards William's grave. He looked at the headstone briefly. 'William Vanderhoof, aged thirty-five years.' The Sheriff shook his head. "So young," he muttered under his breath. "Well, Mr. Vanderhoof, my friend, if there is something to find, we will find it. I'm sorry William, for what is about to ensue." He turned to the other men, "Alright men. Let's get this done."

As if they had just received marching orders, the men grabbed shovels and began digging. The ground hadn't quite had time to freeze over since the burial, and the soil came up easily. With three of them working feverishly, they seemed to be making quick progress. Finally, there was heard the familiar thud of the shovel hitting something below. The wooden coffin box had been reached. And it seemed that it was just in time, too, as the snow had begun falling again and seemed to be getting heavy. The wind had also picked up a bit blowing the ice-cold snow into their faces.

"Alright, men," Sheriff Clarke said mater-of-factly. "We are close. I know you are all cold, and this has been back-breaking work. I am grateful for your help, and once the coffin is on it's way to the coroner, I would ask you to join me for supper at my home."

The digging continued around the box and before long the men had dug around and slightly under the coffin enough to allow for them to lift it slightly and slide a rope around it. Sheriff Clarke grabbed the reigns of the nearby horse, and the opposite end of the rope and tied it around the horn of the saddle. With an urging, via a clicking from his mouth, the horse obeyed and moved forward. The coffin shifted a bit, and you could hear the muffled sound of the body inside of it moving. The men steadied it and helped it to rise. In just a matter of minutes, the coffin was out of the grave and on the snow.

"Alright," Sheriff Clarke said. "Let's get this on the buggy and be on our way."

As the Sheriff slowly pulled away from the cemetery, he looked back over his shoulder. The once pristine snow was now marked with horse tracks and mud. He glanced towards the hole they had just dug and watched as the wind blew the snow into the now-empty grave.

It was two days later after the autopsy had been done by the coroner, Dr. Bonim, when he delivered the stomach, liver, and kidneys to Ann Arbor, Michigan. There waiting, were doctors Palmer and Hendricks, both Professors of Anatomy, and Dr. Prescott, a Professor of Chemistry at the State University. The men had been waiting for the arrival of the organs, as the Sheriff had sent a messenger on ahead. These men had been commissioned with the job to find out if, indeed, there were any traces of poison in the now decomposing body of William Vanderhoof.

The items were carefully carried into the basement of the University, where a science lab had been set up. "Thank you, men," Dr. Prescott said. Please give us until tomorrow, and we will have an opinion."

Back in Galien, Sheriff Clarke paced back and forth in his office, waiting and wondering. He was second-guessing the decision by Mr. Kellogg to keep this quiet from Thomas Vanderhoof. After all, Thomas was a very big member of the community, and he had a lot of influence with others. The waiting was making the Sheriff nervous, and so he decided to leave and get some breakfast when he was met at the door by Thomas Vanderhoof.

"Sheriff!"

"Thomas?"

"Sheriff! Grave robbers have stolen William's body!"

"Thomas come in. Have a seat."

"I was just there! The coffin is gone, and there are tracks from a buggy and at least five horses from what I can tell! Why would someone do this?"

"Thomas, calm down. It is not what you think. There is something that I need to tell you."

"What? What is it?"

"Thomas, please sit." He motioned with his hand to the nearby chair. Thomas removed his black hat and nervously sat down wringing the edge of the hat in his hands.

"Thomas, I have some disturbing news. But, I need you to hear me out first before you jump to any conclusions. Can you do that?"

Slowly, the aged father of William Vanderhoof nodded his head.

Sheriff Clarke drew in a deep breath. "Thomas, Sarah came to see me."

"Sarah? My daughter, Sarah?"

"Yes. She brought me some journals that she had received from the druggist."

"Captain Sterns?"

"Yes. He had asked Sarah to come to see him after William's funeral. And he showed to her two journals that he kept over the years. One was from eighteen hundred seventy-six and the other from eighteen hundred eighty-three. Each of them had an entry in them showing purchases that Elizabeth, William's wife, had made."

"I'm do not understand what you are saying."

"Thomas, the purchase each time was for arsenic."

Thomas' countenance went from frantic with worry to an almost cold hardened stare. "What are you trying to tell me, Mr. Clarke?"

"I'm saying that when I presented the journals to Mr. Kellogg..."

"The Prosecutor? James Kellogg?"

"Yes, please, hear me out. When I presented the journals to Mr. Kellogg, he felt quite strongly that there was enough of a suspicion of wrongdoing around William's death that we should take William's body to the coroner for examination."

"Oh, God! You dug up my son's body!" Thomas jumped up from his seat. "Sheriff, are you saying that you dug up my son's body because you think...." He paused. "Do you think he was poisoned?"

"Thomas, I asked you to hear me through and not get excited. Please, Sir, sit down. There is more."

Thomas plopped back down into the chair as if the weight of the world just landed upon his shoulders.

"The coroner removed the heart, stomach, and kidneys and has delivered them to Ann Arbor for examination by the Scientists of both Anatomy and Chemistry."

"Oh, God! Oh, God!" Thomas repeated with a frantic-like sound to his voice.

"Thomas, the Coroner, consulted with the Doctor and they both believe that William's symptoms are those of arsenic poisoning, and so the organs were delivered to the scientists for further examination before any arrest is made."

"Arrest? Arrest! Who?"

"Thomas, the journal entries, from the druggist, show that it was Elizabeth who purchased the arsenic."

"That's not possible! How could this be possible?" He ran his fingers through his hair. "Are you telling me that Lizzy poisoned him? Is that what you would have me to believe - that my daughter-in-law, mother of my grandchild poisoned my son? Why? Why would she do such a thing?"

"The evidence points in that direction, Thomas."

"Evidence? What evidence? My daughter gives you some journal that the druggist gave her? You know as well as I do that there has always been animosity between her and Lizzy. How do you know she didn't make that up? You know the druggist has always been sweet on her. How is one to know that he didn't do this to gain her favor? Why would he not bring those to you direct?"

"I cannot answer that question. However, after she brought those in, I went to see the doctor. After some discussion, he also agreed that it was worth investigating."

"And neither of you thought to contact me to ask my permission before you dug my son's body out of the ground and created a scandal for my family? My God, Sheriff! Do you have any idea the talk that is going to happen?"

"Thomas, don't you want to know the truth? Don't you want to know if your son was poisoned?"

"And if you are wrong, Sheriff? What then? You just put his body back in the ground minus his organs!?"

"Thomas! We didn't do this lightly. Think about it, Thomas. Think about Nathan Salisbury. Remember him? Don't you remember how he died? I didn't. So I did some investigation into that after Sarah came. He died in the same way, Thomas! And don't you think it coincidental that William had the same symptoms?"

"Coincidental, yes, but you are saying that both of them were poisoned? Would you have me to believe that my daughter-in-law poisoned both of her husbands?"

Sheriff Clarke walked over and placed his hand on Thomas's shoulder. "I understand how upset you are, my friend. But think of William. Don't you think he would expect you to find out if there was a chance? Sarah did the right thing, Thomas. Don't be angry with her. She did it because she loves her brother. If we are right, well, I don't even want to think about that."

"And if you are wrong?"

"Then we can rest assured that we did the best for William. You know him. He would have done the same for you. And there is one more thing."

"There's more? How could there be any more?"

"It's an accusation of a crime. And that will come with an arrest."

Thomas hung his head, and his entire body drooped slightly forward. Slowly he nodded his understanding. "When will we know?"

"Probably tomorrow. And, I know this is asking a great deal from you, but I need you to keep this confidential."

Thomas Vanderhoof stood up. He looked much smaller than the man who had come into the Sheriff's office earlier. His shoulders hung low, weighing him down, and his steps were slow and labored. He walked out into the winter weather toward his waiting team of horses and buggy. Sheriff Clarke stood in the doorway and watched until Thomas was well down the road. Then he shook his head, closed the door, and retreated to the warmth of his office. The snow began to fall heavily as Thomas turned the team down the lane that led to his farm.

Hearing the buggy, Tryphena wiped her hands and pushed the curtains aside. After confirming it was Thomas, she quickly checked the temperature of the stew in the kettle. He would be in shortly, and he always liked his meal to be ready after he had been out. She knew it would be about twenty minutes before he came inside, and when the time had come and gone, and he didn't come inside, she grabbed her grey woolen cape and tromped through the snow to the barn. Inside, she found him sitting on a large bale of hay watching the horses eat.

"Thomas? Are you coming inside?"

"Yes, shortly."

"It was hard to go to the grave. I know," she said, rubbing his shoulder.

"Harder than you know, my dear. Go inside. I will be in shortly."

"Come with me, Thomas. It's cold out here."

"I told you to go inside. I'm fine."

"You don't need to take that tone with me. I was just...."

Thomas stood up. "Yes, you are right. I'm sorry. Let's go inside. We need to talk."

"Thomas? Was is it?"

"Inside, Tryphena, inside." The two walked through the snow back towards the house. Thomas took his time unwrapping his scarf from his neck and plopped down at the table. Tryphena didn't take off her cloak but sat right in front of him with urgency to her look.

"What? What!"

"I went to visit the grave today and ..."

"And what?"

"The body is gone, Tryphena."

"What! What do you mean by saying the body is gone?"

"There has been an accusation of wrongdoing, and the Sheriff had William dug up. They did an autopsy and sent his organs to the University in Ann Arbor."

Her mouth hung open as if she couldn't believe what was being told to her. The words that came out of her next were slow, "What are you saying, Thomas?"

"They have reason to believe that Willie was poisoned."

She gasped. "Who's they?"

"The Sheriff and the Prosecutor."

"Prosecutor? Oh, God, Thomas! What has happened?" she sat back. Her eyes darted wildly around the room. She looked up at Thomas for some sense of normalcy to the discussion, but Thomas was looking away, staring towards the stove fire. "Whatever shall we do?"

"What do you mean – what shall we do?" he responded.

"If they find poison, I mean. What if they find poison?"

"I pray to Almighty God that they don't. I pray to God that they don't," he repeated. Standing up, he said, "I'm sorry dear, but I'm not hungry, and I do not wish to speak of this any longer. I wish to go lie down." As he walked away, he stopped abruptly. "And Tryphena, you are not to speak a word about this to anyone!"

"How can you say for me to not speak of it? You cannot just say something of this degree and not speak of it. Why it is...."

"Tryphena! Please! That's enough!"

"Yes, Thomas. I apologize. Of course." She busied herself about the kitchen, thinking about the news she had just heard. She was worried, and that worry kept her up throughout the evening. Early morning came two days later when she was out feeding the chickens as the Sheriff's buggy pulled down the lane. He had his deputy with him.

"Ma'am? Is Thomas around?"

"He's in the barn," she said nervously.

As the Sheriff disembarked from the buggy, she couldn't help but follow him. Thomas was at the grinding wheel, sharpening his ax as he saw the Sheriff walk in. In almost slow motion, the grinding wheel came to a halt, and he stood up.

"Sheriff?"

"Thomas. Can we go inside?"

"Yes, yes, of course." The walk back towards the house, although a short distance, seemed to take a long time. The three walked in silence.

"Sheriff Clarke?" Thomas questioned after removing his coat and standing near the table. He eagerly waited for the Sheriff to begin speaking.

"Thomas, I regret to have to tell you this, but the tests came back positive. They show that William had a significant amount of arsenic in his body. It appears that your son was, indeed, poisoned."

Thomas' legs suddenly felt weak, and he grabbed at the chair next to him. Choking back tears, he said, "And what of my grandchildren?"

"Your grandchildren? What do you mean-what of your grandchildren?" Tryphena interjected. "Oh my!" The light suddenly went off in her head as she stumbled through the next few words. "You think Lizzy poisoned him?" She looked frantically over towards her husband and then back towards the Sheriff. "You think Lizzy poisoned him?" she repeated.

Sheriff Clarke spoke, "The evidence points in that direction. We are going there now. Thomas, I have come to ask you if you would like to take possession of the children or if you would like me to bring them to Lizzy's mother?"

He spoke in a whisper as if speaking was a chore. He nodded. "I will come to get the children."

Chapter 6
Indianapolis

The sun was beginning to rise when Doug and Robert reached Indianapolis. Suddenly everything seemed to get very somber as the men pulled up towards the Federal building. After going around and around in the parking garage, Robert finally found a space suitable to his liking. His silver Jeep came to a stop, and he turned off the engine. Doug quickly reached for the door, but Robert didn't move.

"What's the matter?" Doug asked.

"I don't know. I just have a really bad feeling about Lynn. I mean I haven't heard anything about her, the police haven't been very helpful. Now, this."

"I get it. You're scared."

"Hell yes, I'm scared! My wife is missing! What if they think I had something to do with it?"

"Did you?"

Robert shot Doug a disgusted look. "No! I didn't have anything to do with it!"

"Then you don't have anything to worry about."

"But what if they think I did? And what if they think I'm making all of this up? I mean, she has been hiding stuff all over the place like some damn detective movie! People are breaking into my house!"

Doug stopped him. "We'll find her."

Robert was silent for a moment. Then he looked at Doug with tears welling up in his eyes. "What if she's dead?"

"No, don't say that. She's not dead. You know I've always had a sixth sense. I just know it. She's not dead."

"I hope you're right." He reached for the latch on his vehicle, and the pair began the walk towards the parking garage elevators. As they did, another vehicle slowly entered the parking garage.

After initial security precautions, the two were taken down a long hall to a waiting room. The quietness and almost eerie setting inside the building seemed to rattle Doug a bit, but Robert was distant and almost robotic.

"Someone's finally coming," Doug said, sitting up a bit straighter. In the distance, they could hear shoes clicking on the floor. Whoever it was seemed to be walking with a sense of urgency. And then they stopped. Muffled talking took place outside the door, and as quick as it had started, it stopped. The door opened. In walked not one, but two FBI agents. The first agent was tall and slender, a bit older than the other, and graying around the temples. The second was also slender but shorter and younger. The second one stood off to the side of the table, while the older man sat down.

"Gentleman, I am agent Harvey, and this is agent Marle. Which of you two men was I speaking with last night on the phone?"

Slowly Robert raised his hand.

"And your name again?"

"Robert Willis."

The Agent clicked on his pen and began scratching on a sheet of paper. "So let's go through this again. Start from the beginning and tell me what has been happening?"

Robert began the slow, almost painful, story of what had transpired over the last several days. He paused at times as he became a bit overwhelmed with emotion, and the detective had to keep urging him on. When he got to the part about the detective named Maggie Martin, the officer that was standing straightened his stance and stepped forward.

"You are positive she said her name was Maggie Martin?"

"Yes, why?"

Agent Harvey raised his hand as if motioning for the current conversation to halt, and then added, "Mr. Willis, we do not have a Maggie Martin here."

Robert interrupted, "So we are at the wrong branch? Why did you have me drive all this way? You specifically told me to come here. Why would you do that if she wasn't at this branch?"

"If you will let me continue, Sir." The detective reached into the folder that he had beneath his legal pad and pulled out a photo. "Is this anyone you recognize?" The photo was of a short, thin blue-eyed, woman with dark hair. She was holding a plaque at some type of ceremony.

"No, I don't recognize her, should I?"

"This was Agent Maggie Martin. She was killed in the line of duty two years ago. Can you describe what this person, who called herself Maggie Martin, looked like?"

"Umm...she was short, blonde, maybe one hundred thirty-five pounds."

"You say she has been to your home? Did she use any form of identification?"

"I don't recall, maybe, wait, yes, she did."

Doug interjected, "So what you are saying is that someone is impersonating an FBI agent?"

The detective's phone buzzed. Looking down at it, he said, "Excuse us for a moment, would you please?" The two detectives walked out abruptly, leaving Robert and Doug in their wake.

Once outside the room, Detective Harvey walked next door into another room. There standing in front of a one-way glass mirror was a woman. She was about five feet six inches tall, slender and with dark hair that was pulled back tightly into a ponytail. She had a cup of coffee in her right hand, and without turning to look at Detective Harvey, she said, "I am concerned for his safety. We need to shut this operation down and end this."

"Shut it down? What? I'm not shutting this down."

"I don't like it!"

"Like or don't like — it is not an option in our line of work! Don't get your personal feelings and your professional obligation mixed up! You knew what you were signing up for."

The dark-haired woman spun around. "Don't push me, Harvey. Yes, I knew what I was signing up for! But I didn't know it was going to go this far."

He took a step closer. His voice softened. "Look, I know this is hard for you. We are close to getting what we want and who we want. He won't get hurt. I promise you."

"How do you know that?"

"I have my guys on him. He has been under surveillance."

"Can you assure me that neither of these innocent men will come to harm? Can you assure me of that?"

Harvey took the coffee cup from her hand and took a sip out of it, "I will try to wrap this up in the next few days. In the meantime, I think I am going to have you re-assigned."

The woman became indignant. "You will do no such thing! You are where you are in this operation because of me, and you know it. Don't you dare try to pull me off!"

He took another sip of the coffee. "Then I suggest you get your head back in the game." He handed the cup back to her and walked away. Slowly, she turned back towards the one-way glass window.

Inside the room, Doug turned towards Robert, "Holy crap! This is getting deep! What was your wife into? Man, I'm scared!"

"Me too, Doug. Me too."

"Don't go back to your place. You can stay with us."

"I don't know. I...."

"No, seriously, Robert. Your wife stirred up a hornet's nest, and I don't think you are safe."

At that moment Detectives Harley and Marle returned. "Mr. Willis?" Agent Harvey addressed Robert. "I am going to have to speak to you privately, if I may."

"Not a chance," Robert said. "Doug can hear whatever you need to say to me."

Agent Harvey looked over at Agent Marle and back at Robert again. Then he leaned back in his chair. "Alright, gentlemen, if that is the way you wish to play this."

"We aren't playing anything, Sir," Robert interrupted. "We came here for help. My wife is missing. Someone has been in my home. Now you are telling me the police or the detective or whoever the hell it is - is not really who she says she is. No, Sir. I'm not the one playing, but the one that is being played. So if you don't mind, I would appreciate you telling me exactly what the hell is going on."

Doug let out a breathy whistle and smoothed back the top of his hair. The detective took in a deep breath and sat forward.

"Alright, Mr. Willis. Here is what I can tell you. Yes, I know your wife is missing. And yes, I am aware that she was being followed."

"How?"

"We received this about two weeks ago in the mail." He slipped an envelope forward that he pulled out of the Manila folder. Robert gingerly opened it up. There were several items, including photos and an old newspaper article about the Vanderhoof trial. There was also a handwritten note from Lynn. It simply read, 'you wanted proof, here's proof.'

"I'm not following you, Sir. What is all of this?" Robert said, putting down the photo.

"Your wife had contacted us a while back and told us that she had come across something illegal and that she was being followed. After speaking with her, and since it was from over one hundred thirty-five years ago, I informed her that there was nothing I could do, and if she believed there to be something illegal, then I would need proof. Well, as you can imagine, knowing your wife, the conversation didn't go well and ..." He paused.

"And what!"

"She hung up on me, and then these showed up. When I attempted to contact her ..." Again he paused.

84

"When you attempted to contact her...then what!"

"We were not able to get in touch, so I dispatched a few agents and through our contacts, found out she was missing. But that is not all."

"God! How could there be more? What the hell is wrong with you people? A woman tells you she is being followed, and you dismiss her as a lunatic? You don't even bother to send the police out to investigate?"

"Sir, if you would let me continue."

"Oh, please do! This situation couldn't get any deeper steeped in shit than it is now!"

The detective took in a deep breath as if he was getting annoyed. "We did send the police. And we have an inside person, but it is not the person you describe. Our person is not the one you know as Maggie Martin."

"Meaning?"

"Meaning, your wife did go to the police, and that is when she disappeared."

"She was at the police station?" Doug jumped in on the conversation.

The detective changed his glance from Robert over to Doug, "She was. In fact, my agent was there at the time."

"So, what does that mean?"

"That is what we are working to find out. We know she didn't leave the station, at least not the way she came in. My agent would have seen that."

Robert sat back, stunned. He went to pull out his vaporizer but realized it was still back at security where it had been confiscated when he and Doug arrived. He sat back, staring at the detective and shaking his head slightly up and down in a sort of nod. Then he abruptly stood up pushing his chair out from under him with a loud screeching. He paced back and forth like a lion in a cage.

"Mr. Willis, please, sit down. I'm going to need you to sit down."

Robert interrupted him, "What I need to know right now and right here is if my wife is alive. Tell me, Detective! Is she alive?"

Detective Harvey looked over at detective Marle, and from behind the one-way glass, the other agent held her breath.

Chapter 7
The Arrest

Back in Galien, 1884

"Do you suppose we will get a storm this evening?" Elizabeth questioned John as the two were out in the barn cleaning stalls and feeding the animals.

"From the looks of that sky, it seems likely," he responded. "We best put out some extra bedding for the animals."

"Would you be able to bring some wood into the house also, John?"

"Yes, certainly," he looked at her and winked.

"Oh, John. What would I do without you?" She smiled in his direction.

He dropped his pitchfork and walked over towards her. "I'm sure you would manage somehow. My guess is you would flash those crystal blue eyes in the direction of some unsuspecting man and ..." He grabbed her around the waist and pulled her towards him.

"Don't you get fresh with me, Mr. Chapman!" she laughed. "Now come on inside for some supper."

Releasing his grip on her, he added, "I have a few things yet to do. I will be up there shortly."

Lizzy opened the large door as the wind blew its way into the barn kicking up some straw on the floor. As she turned around to head towards the house, she heard the familiar noise of a team of horses, and the creaking of a wagon drawing near. She glanced down the road, but as the snow had begun to fall quite thickly, she couldn't quite make out who it was because they were still a short distance off. But the more she looked, she could tell that there was more than one wagon. Not thinking much about either since she wasn't the only home along that road, she gathered her dress up so the snow wouldn't soak the bottom of it, and began trudging back up the path towards the house. It had been a snowy winter thus far, and there was a good layer of snow along the path, making it a bit treacherous and slow going. She would be happy for the spring to arrive finally.

Making the turn onto her property and driving up the path slowly behind her was the wagon with its unknown riders. She stopped, and before long, the first wagon was alongside her. She looked up. It was Thomas Vanderhoof.

"Thomas? I didn't expect you today. What are you doing out on such a day as this? And Tryphena? How did he talk you out on this winter day?" she joked.

"I didn't expect to come today," he replied. "Whoa," he signaled to the team who obeyed upon command.

"You are welcome to stay for supper and put the horses in the barn for a bit. John is in there now. He could help unhitch the team. The girls will be glad to see you."

"No, thank you. We won't be staying long."

"Put the horses in the barn anyhow, and I will get some tea for us. Who is that coming behind you?"

Thomas said nothing but disembarked from the wagon and reached up to grab hold of Tryphena's hand. Tryphena had a difficult time looking at Lizzy because she knew the real purpose of their visit. She quickly climbed the stairs to the home and went inside to see the girls.

The noise of the rustling wagons had caught the attention of John, and he had begun making his way back towards the house just as the Sheriff's wagon came to a halt behind Thomas' team. Seeing Thomas Vanderhoof and Sheriff Clarke, John slowed his pace a bit.

The Sheriff climbed down and faced Elizabeth. "Mrs. Vanderhoof," he addressed her.

"Sheriff?" Lizzy questioned.

"Ma'am, may we go inside?" Looking over towards John, he added, "Mr. Chapman, please join us."

Lizzy glanced quizzically at John and then climbed up the stairs into the house.

Deputy Brown walked around the back of the group and behind John Chapman. Once inside, Elizabeth's eyes darted from Thomas to Tryphena and then over at the Sheriff. "What is it? Is something wrong?"

Upon seeing Thomas, Lydia ran over to him to hug him. "Grandpa Vanderhoof!"

"Hello, my little ladybug!" He scooped her up and kissed her on the forehead. "Would you do Grandpa a really big favor?"

"Yes, anything!"

"Please take your sister and go upstairs to your room and close the door. We are going to have a conversation down here, okay?"

"Okay," she responded, slightly disappointed. He kissed her again on the forehead and placed her down on the floor. His eyes began to fill with tears, but he quickly regained his composure as he sat down at the table and unbuttoned his woolen coat. Tryphena stood behind him, not saying a word but staring at the Sheriff. Her hand was on Thomas's shoulder, and her uneasiness manifested itself.

Glancing at Thomas and then Tryphena, Lizzy became nervous, "Thomas? Tryphena? What's wrong?" Thomas said nothing but hung his head so not make eye contact with her.

The Sheriff took in a deep breath. His heavy leather boots made a solid sound upon the wooden floor as he stepped up to her. "Elizabeth there has been an accusation."

"What do you mean, an accusation?"

"About William's death. The accusation is that he was poisoned."

"Poisoned? You are talking foolishly! William died from a weakened heart. The doctor stated such. Both doctors stated such."

"Elizabeth, we have pulled up the body."

She recoiled in an almost horrified manner. "You pulled up the body? Do you mean you dug him from the grave?"

"Yes, that is what I mean."

Oh, my God! What? Why?"

The Sheriff continued, "There was an autopsy done, and there was evidence of poisoning."

"I...I don't understand. How could that be? How could he have been poisoned?"

"Elizabeth, I am here on official duty."

"What official duty? What are you talking about?"

The Sheriff cleared his throat and continued, "Elizabeth Vanderhoof, you are under arrest for the murder of your husband, William."

"What! What are you saying? Do you think I poisoned Willie?" She recoiled in horror.

The deputy stood behind John and in front of the door that led to the outside. He stepped forward and took John by the arm. "John Chapman, you are under arrest for the murder of William Vanderhoof."

"Get your hands off me!" he said to the deputy and shook his arm free. "I don't know what you are talking about, but I didn't murder anyone!"

"Thomas! Thomas! What's going on?" Lizzy began to raise her voice in a fevered pitch. "How could I murder him? Tell them, Thomas! Tell them I didn't kill Willie!"

But Thomas said nothing. He looked up at her with tears now forming in his eyes and just stared at her in silence.

"Sheriff, please!" she continued. "There must be some type of error. I swear I didn't do such a thing! I loved him!" Her loud pleading caught the attention of her daughter upstairs, who now had opened the upstairs door wide enough to hear part of the conversation. Lydia inched her way out and was standing at the end of the stairway. Hearing her mother begging frightened her, and she ran down the stairs to her mother and threw her arms around her legs.

"Lydia! Come here, child!" Thomas called to her, but she didn't obey. She was clinging to her mother, and now crying because she was frightened. Tryphena walked over and grabbed hold of Lydia and pulled her away.

"Mama! Mama!" she screamed.

"Sheriff, please, you have to believe me! I did not harm my husband! Please, don't do this! My children! My children!"

Tryphena said to the little girl, "Go upstairs, child, immediately, and gather your things. You and your sister are coming with us."

"No, No! Mama!" Lydia's scream was intensifying.

Elizabeth was frantic and wiggling. The Sheriff had a good hold of her. "No, you are not taking my children! You did this, Tryphena didn't you! You did this to me! You hate me this much? And why, because Willie turned down your advances? Do you think I don't know? You poisoned him, didn't you! You gave him the medicine the night that he died!" You did this, and you have blamed me!"

Thomas looked up and over at Tryphena, then back at Lydia. Do as you are told! Get your things and come back down here immediately!"

"What right do you have, Sheriff," John added. "to do such a thing without evidence! To do such a thing in front of these children!"

"I have every right, Mr. Chapman. We have evidence."

"Evidence?" Lizzy shouted. "What evidence?"

"We had the body examined, Lizzy."

"What are you talking about! What did you have examined?"

"He had arsenic in his body, Lizzy."

"Arsenic? And you think I put it there? By what proof? How dare you come into my home and frighten my children! What proof do you have that I put arsenic into his body?"

"Let's go! You will get a fair trial."

"Trial! Sheriff! Please! Stop! At least let me get my bag and my Bible!" The Sheriff sent Tryphena for those items as Lizzy continued to plead with him. He led her outside towards the waiting team. She dug her heels into the snow and would not get up into the buggy. She began to strike him in an attempt to get free.

"Do not force me to tie your hands, Lizzy." He reached down and picked her up.

Meanwhile inside, Thomas got up from the table and walked across to John. He stood in front of him, staring into his eyes. "You have robbed me of my son and robbed my grandchild of her father. You will pay for what you have done."

"I did nothing to you or your son. I am just a hired hand. You have nothing on me." He turned his attention to the deputy. "You have no reason to hold me, Sir."

Thomas grabbed hold of John's coat, "I will see you hang."

John pushed Thomas backward, "Not likely. Get your hands off me." The deputy quickly grabbed John's arms and walked him out the door and into the cold waiting wagon where Elizabeth was inside staring blankly at the ground. Her eyes were still wet from tears. John took a seat next to her, but she didn't move or even look at him. She was distant.

"Lizzy, we will get out of this," he reassured. "There's no proof. None." Still, she didn't respond. The Sheriff cued the team, and slowly they pulled away from the white farmhouse, leaving her children and all that she had behind.

Back inside, Thomas walked slowly up the stairs. With each step, the heaviness of his feet could be heard by the girls who were upstairs crying. Opening the door, he walked over towards the bed and sat down. "Girls, come here." Nervously they obeyed.

"I want to apologize if I raised my voice and frightened you. You know I love you very much." He reached around and put his arms around them.

"Where did the Sheriff take Mama?" Lydia asked

"The Sheriff took your Mama and Mr. Chapman to jail."

Janie began crying. "But why? Why, Grandpa?"

"You are big enough to know. The Sheriff believes your Mama and Mr. Chapman may have had something to do with your papa's death. I'm sorry to tell you this, child. But you are going to come to live with us for a while until this whole thing is straightened out. It will be okay. I will look after you."

"I want to see my Grandma," Lydia cried. "I want to see Grandma Hardy."

"Yes. You will go stay with grandmother Hardy."

"Me too?" Janie asked.

"No, Janie. You are coming with me."

"But I want to be with Lydia."

"Again, I'm sorry, child. Lydia belongs there, and you belong with me. That is the way it is. Now, I need you to gather some things, and we can be on our way."

Tryphena was downstairs waiting. She had tried to busy herself to keep the nervousness of her mood in check. She put away all the food and prepared the house to be closed up for a bit. Seeing the group finally coming down the stairs, she hurried over to them. "We're not going to be able to leave just yet. Look! The snow is coming down hard now. We may need to spend the evening here."

Thomas looked out the window and over at the team. Yes, it was snowing hard, and he didn't want to take a chance with the children out in the weather. "I will put the team in the barn for the night. Tryphena, would you please fix something for us to eat?"

He trudged out into the snow and led the horses towards the barn. There was an empty stall at the far end of the barn, so he worked to get fresh straw down and unhitch the team. He looked around the barn. At the other end was the prize horse that he had given to William for breeding. And then there was the other team of horses that he had helped William train to pull the buggy. Memories flooded his mind. He walked over and petted the horses on the nose. Tears again welled in his eyes. In desperation to stop the emotions that were flooding his being, he looked up toward the rafters, as if looking up to heaven itself. But he could no longer contain himself as the weight of the events came crashing down upon him. He began to sob. And the more he tried to stop, the more he cried. So much in fact that he began to feel weak and walked over to a hay bale and sat down. That was when he noticed a leather bag in the stall next to him. It was an odd-looking bag. Almost as if it was military issued. He wiped his eyes and walked over and picked it up. Quickly, he recognized that the contents inside must belong to John Chapman. He went through them, and that is when he found a picture. It was of John and some other soldiers. He looked at the photo for a while, and then he saw it. The man standing next to John in the photo was Nathan Salisbury, Lizzy's first husband.

He was slightly confused. Thoughts raced through his head. Frantically, he dumped out the canvas bag onto the ground in front of him. He dug through them, studying each thing he found. Inside a tied handkerchief he found a golden pocket watch. It was beautiful and etched with the initials JC. He clicked it open and could not believe what was in front of his own eyes – a small picture cut down enough to fit inside the opening of the watch. The picture was crinkled along the edges as if the watch was opened and closed many times upon it. But there was no mistaking who the photo inside was. It was Elizabeth – a younger version of her, but definitely Elizabeth.

Chapter 8
Shelter at Redding Mill

The wind was blowing the snow about fiercely as the wagon carried John and Elizabeth towards town and the jail cell that awaited them. Elizabeth hadn't said a word since getting into the wagon and had continued to stare with a blank, almost empty gaze in her eyes.

The deputy had been staring at Elizabeth and suddenly fixated upon her abdomen. He wasn't sure, but it looked as if she was expecting a child. Noticing him staring at her, she locked eyes with him. The dark black emptiness of her eyes made him suddenly uncomfortable, and he looked away.

It was nearing suppertime when the Sheriff decided that the weather was just too bad to continue to push the horses, and he stopped at Jonah Redding's Mill. The mill was not currently in operation since Jonah had passed away suddenly last year, but there were several buildings there, including a barn, and the property was tied to the Redding home, just up the hill behind it. The Sheriff sent the deputy up the back hill to alert Mrs. Redding that they were going to take shelter in the barn for the night. After struggling to open the large barn doors, Sheriff Clarke walked the team inside.

"Alright, I think we will let Lizzy sleep inside the wagon, and the rest of us can sleep out here in this stall."

"Are you crazy, Sheriff? You expect a woman to sleep in a barn? She'll freeze to death!"

"She won't freeze to death. This is a good solid barn, and we have blankets for the horses. We can use those."

"That is indecent, Sheriff!"

"So was killing her husband," a voice came from behind. The deputy had just arrived back at the barn, and he had a lantern, some bread, and three large blankets.

"You take that back!" John moved toward him.

Sheriff Clarke grabbed his gun. "There will be none of that, Mr. Chapman. Now, get over there in that corner. Deputy, tie his hands in front of him with that rope over there and then tie it to the post. Leave enough length so he can lie down."

Looking over at Elizabeth who was still sitting in the back of the wagon, he waved his gun and continued, "Don't think for one moment that I won't use this on either of you. It's my job to bring both of you in for trial, and that is what I intend to do!"

Without saying a word, Elizabeth worked her way toward the step and climbed down. She walked up to the Sheriff's Deputy and took a blanket from him, then walked over to where John was sitting in the stall and sat down next to him. She pulled the blanket over them both and lay down with her head upon a broken pile of straw. The deputy looked over at her and John and then over at the Sheriff. He spit upon the ground and then walked over to unhitch the team of horses.

John scooted closer and pushed his shoulder into hers as if to get her attention. "Lizzy, it will all be okay. We will get this worked out. The girls will be fine for a night or two. Thomas will see to it." Still, she did not respond.

Darkness began to take over the interior of the barn, and the Sheriff finally lit the kerosene lamp that Mrs. Redding had sent down with the Deputy. "Do you want the first watch or the second?" he asked the Deputy.

"I'll take the first," came the reply.

Elizabeth turned on her side and closed her eyes. John did the same while facing her, staring at her for some time before his eyes began to grow heavy, and he finally fell asleep. It was late into the night when she awoke. She looked at John and then over at the Sheriff who was sitting up sleeping. Nudging him roughly, he opened his eyes. "Roll onto your back and move very close to me," she whispered into his ear. He quickly obeyed. Leaning in very close, she said, "We must not tell them we are married."

"Why's that?" he whispered back.

"That will add to their ammunition, John. They will say that we wanted William out of the way so that we could be together. Promise me you will not say anything about it."

"I will do as you ask."

"Good. I believe the deputy thinks I am expecting a child. I saw it in his eyes. I plan to use that to my advantage to be released."

"And what of me, Lizzy?"

"There is no reason in the world for them to have arrested you. I am almost sure that Sarah had something to do with that since you spoke so sharply to her. You will be released. It's me they are after."

"What if they don't release you, Lizzy?"

"I don't want to think in that matter, John. Just remember your promise." She grabbed his hand beneath the blanket and closed her eyes.

When morning came, the snow had ceased, and there was a fresh thick layer across the land. The barn door opened and in walked Mrs. Redding. "Sheriff, I thought you might want…". She paused when she saw Elizabeth.

"Elizabeth? What are you doing here?" Turning to the Sheriff, she continued, "Sheriff, I had no idea you were traveling with Mrs. Vanderhoof." She scurried over to Lizzy. "My dear, I had no idea you were with them. You should have stayed in the house and …"

She stopped. "Why are you with them, dear? Sheriff?"

"Thank you for your hospitality, Mrs. Redding. We will be on our way."

"Sheriff Clarke! What is the exact meaning of this? Lizzy are you okay, dear?"

"Mrs. Redding! We appreciate your great hospitality, but now you are interfering with the law. So, if you don't mind, we will be hitching the team up and moving on."

"I most certainly do mind! How dare you treat a lady in such a manner! Come, dear, let's get you into some warmer clothes."

"I'm afraid I cannot let you do that, Ma'am," the Deputy chimed in. "She and Mr. Chapman are under arrest."

"Arrest? For what? This is absurd!"

"She's under arrest for the murder of her husband!"

Mrs. Redding's mouth dropped open, and she looked over at Lizzy and then at John. "Is it true, dear? What they say, I mean. Is it true?"

Lizzy said nothing but John spoke loudly, "No, it isn't true! Somehow they got it into their heads that Lizzy killed her husband and dragged her out of her home in front of her children, and here we are in a cold barn like animals!"

"Quiet down over there," Sheriff Clarke ordered.

"Why should I, Sheriff? Don't you want Mrs. Redding here to know the truth as to how you have injured Mrs. Vanderhoof based on no evidence?"

"I said that is enough. Deputy, get them into the wagon. Mrs. Redding, thank you again and good day to you, Ma'am."

Hazel Redding watched helplessly as both John and Elizabeth were escorted back into the wagon. "Lizzy, the children? Where are the children?"

"The children are taken care of Mrs. Redding, now if you don't mind, please get out of the way," The Sheriff was getting annoyed.

Hazel Redding obeyed and turned towards her home. She walked as quickly as she could up the hill to fetch her winter clothing. She was going on a short trip to see Thomas Vanderhoof. He would know what to do.

As the wagon pulled up in front of the station, there wasn't much action in town. John didn't say a word but jumped down when the Deputy urged him.

Expecting to have a struggle with Elizabeth, the Sheriff fastened his hat a bit more on his head and approached her. Again, without speaking or fussing, she stepped down and walked into the jail on her own. Once inside, she took a brief look around and then walked over to the cell where John had just been placed. It was empty except for a thin mattress upon the cot and a chair in the corner. The Sheriff opened the cell door, and she walked inside. Before she had an opportunity to turn around, the Sheriff closed and locked it.

"My apologies, Ma'am. I do not have separate quarters. We are not used to having women in here. You'll both have to stay in there together, which didn't seem to bother you too much last night. I'll get another cot and a few blankets. Make yourself comfortable. We are waiting on the Judge. He could be here tomorrow or the next day, depending on the weather."

"Look, Sheriff," John spoke up. "I don't mind waiting here for a day or two for the Judge to show up, but isn't there someplace she could be other than here until then?"

"No. All prisoners stay here until the Judge decides when the trial will be." Sheriff Clarke walked over to a large bureau that was on the opposite side of the room. Pulling out two blankets and a pillow, he then shoved them through the bars. Elizabeth watched them fall to the ground. "Now, are either of you hungry? Because I would sure like to get home, get some fresh boots, and some sleep." Neither of the prisoners spoke up. "Alright then, Deputy, I will be back later. I'm going to feed and rest the team, and get some rest myself."

The Deputy took his place behind the Sheriff's desk, and John walked over and sat next to Lizzy. She was shivering. Placing a blanket around her, he whispered into her ear, "It will be okay. Trust me."

Slowly she turned to him, and their eyes met. There was a coldness there. A coldness he had seen once before.

Chapter 9
Questions

Thomas had tossed and turned all night. At times, he watched Tryphena sleep, at others, he opened the watch and stared at the photo inside and wondered, and still at other times, he prayed silently. He prayed that God would reveal the truth of his son's death. He prayed that God would keep him from becoming angry and bitter. He prayed that the girls would find comfort in their heart apart from the terrible scene that they witnessed last evening. And then there was the prayer for Tryphena. The words of Lizzy's accusation rang in his head - 'Just because Willie turned away your advances?' Over and over, he kept thinking about it. He had not questioned her immediately upon returning to the house after his trip to the barn. It wasn't the time. But there would be a time, and he would ask. Oh, yes, he would ask.

As the morning sun rose in the east, he donned his black woolen coat and headed off towards the barn to care for the horses. As he tramped through the freshly fallen snow, he looked around at the property. The property he had wanted years ago that the Matthew Salisbury, Nathan's father, had staked a claim to and purchased ahead of him. It is what had started the rivalry between the two families. The river that ran through the property was the same one that used to run the Redding Mill on the opposite side of the county, and Thomas had wanted to start a mill many years ago. Somehow Nathan's father had made a deal for the Indian land, and Thomas never had a chance. The Salisbury family had grabbed up quite a bit of land and had become a very wealthy family. After the death of both Nathan and his father, Elizabeth was now in control of the property and all the estate.

Thomas had been against William going to work for Nathan Salisbury after the war. No son of his was going to work to enrich the Salisbury family. But William had other plans. And as Thomas began watering the horses, the conversation that he and William had eight years ago began to flood his mind.

*****

"You will do no such thing, William! No son of mine will work for that family! The same family that robbed me of the land that I was attempting to purchase! The family that went behind my back to file the deed!"

"Father, I ask that you take inventory of your feelings! You forget that I am an adult. Please, do not shout at me. I have only intentions for the betterment of our family. I ask that you hear me out."

"And are you forgetting to whom you are speaking?"

"Maybe so, Father. But please listen to me. You will be interested in what I have to say."

"Will I now? And what is that?"

"Well, as you know, I served with Nathan during the war. I spent many a day walking next to him or talking with him at camp during the nights. I was there when he took a bullet to his spine and became cripple."

"Why is that of any consequence, William?"

104

"Because I found out something else. Something that may allow us to get the property."

Thomas looked at his son, quizzically. "I'm listening."

One night, we were all at camp, and it was raining mighty heavy. I remember walking through the muddy ground towards the doctor's tent because I had a really bad toothache. I was just about to pull open the flap when I heard voices coming from the inside. I recognized the doctor's voice, and the other voice I recognized to be that of Nathan Salisbury. The doctor was telling him that his lungs sounded bad, really bad. Said he had some lung disease. Said he didn't know if there was a treatment for it. Nathan asked the doctor how long he thought he would live. The doctor told him that he couldn't be sure, but maybe a year or two."

Thomas sat down on the chair nearby and listened intently. "I'm not sure what your point is, William. We all knew Nathan was sick when he returned from the war."

"Yes, but someone will be needed to help around the farm. Someone will need to be sure the Widow Salisbury is taken care of."

"William! Are you suggesting what I think you are suggesting? That is preposterous!"

"And why is that? Elizabeth Salisbury will need help with the farm. She won't be able to do it herself. Do you think a beautiful young woman like that will not want to marry again?"

"Marry! William!"

"If we married, I wouldn't just get the widow, Father. I would get the property, too. We could sell off the northern acreage, about seventy-five acres, to you for the mill."

"William, that is dishonest."

"Dishonest? How? I'm not creating a scandal. I would be marrying the widow. Isn't that what Tryphena and you did?"

★★★★

Thomas' mind came back to reality at the thought of Tryphena and the words that Lizzy had spoken the night before. Tryphena was much younger than him, and it wasn't long after they were married when Thomas realized how much he loved her. He had thought all this time that she loved him too, but Lizzy's words that she spoke the night of the arrest kept haunting him.

"Thomas!" The loud call startled him. It was his wife. "Didn't you hear me call you? I have the children ready to go. Is the team ready?"

"Yes, the team is ready. I will be up to the house in a bit. I want to be sure the rest of these animals have what they need."

The ride back towards his farm was cold. The wind had stopped blowing, but the air was frigid.

"I'm going to need to see Mrs. Hardy today." He was, of course, referring to Nancy Hardy, Elizabeth's mother.

"Yes, yes, of course."

"If you prefer, I can drop you and the girls at the house and go on to speak with her in private. She can come for Lydia after that."

"Do what you think is best. I don't understand why we cannot take both of the girls with us."

"Jane is Willie's daughter, and Lydia belonged to Nathan. You know this. Why are you questioning me? This is hard for me, too."

"Then, why do it? Why, Thomas?"

He turned in an odd fashion and said, "Why indeed, Tryphena? Maybe the question should be asked of you."

"Me? Whatever do you mean?"

"I am referring to Lizzy's comments. What did she mean when she spoke of advances?"

"Thomas, do not insult me by talking of such a thing in front of the children. If you have information that you require of me, we can discuss that in private!"

He took the correction and soon the group arrived home to find Sarah and Mrs. Redding sitting at the table. Seeing Thomas, Sarah jumped up. "Father! Mrs. Redding tells me that they have arrested Lizzy?! Is it true?"

"Girls go upstairs," He said, motioning to Jane and Lydia. Then he turned to Sarah. "How dare you speak of such a thing in front of those children! And how dare you not act as if you knew nothing of this! Why Sarah? Why did you not come to me first? Do I not have the respect of my daughter that she would come to me with such accusations?" He walked over and towards the stove, took off his coat and warmed his hands. Then he walked back over towards the table. "Mrs. Redding, I apologize for my outburst. As you may be able to infer, I have had a difficult evening."

"Mr. Vanderhoof, there is no need to apologize. I came as soon as I could get here. It is awful the way Lizzy was treated by being kept in the barn and all."

"To what are you referring, Mrs. Redding?"

"They stayed in my barn last night. The Sheriff, Deputy, Lizzy, and the other man. I am not familiar with him."

"John Chapman, no doubt," Sarah said snidely.

"Sarah, you will mind your manners while you are in my home!"

Mrs. Redding continued, "I was just so worried about Lizzy. It does not fit for a woman to be in a barn with three men all night. I came to talk to you about that, Thomas, but you were not here. Is it true? Have they arrested her?"

"It is true," Tryphena interjected. "Mrs. Redding, I want to thank you for coming. But as you can tell, Thomas needs some rest. I do not wish to insult you, but I would like to continue this visit at a later date."

"Yes, yes, of course, dear. I,...I am sorry...about Lizzy and of course about William. You know you will be in my prayers. Good afternoon."

Sarah was putting on her cloak to walk out with the widow when Thomas spoke up. "Sarah, I wish to speak with you in private. Tryphena, dear, please see what the girls are doing. Turning to his daughter, he demanded, "Sarah Joy, you will explain yourself to me! Why have you brought such shame to this family?"

"Shame? Shame! Father, how have I brought shame to this family? It is Elizabeth who has brought shame to this family!"

"You are a fool, Sarah!. You have no idea about your brother or your brother's affairs. If you had such a suspicion, you should have come to me first!"

"Why would I not go to the Sheriff? I have evidence that Willie was murdered and...."

"Suspicion! You have suspicion! You have created a scandal for William, Elizabeth, and our family based on your suspicion! Not to speak of the destruction of those little girls!"

Sarah stood up indignantly. "You may refer to it as suspicion if you want, Father. I will call it what it was – murder! Plain and simple murder! One would think you would not be feeling so sorry for Lizzy if she is the person responsible for killing Willie! But instead, you have turned your hostility towards me. That is completely unfounded, and I will not be insulted in such a manner! No, I did not come to you, and for that, I do apologize. I was waiting to hear from the Sheriff as to what Mr. Kellogg would say. How was I to know that they had acted upon my suspicion? I did not want to worry you unnecessarily, Father."

His voice softened. "Sarah, please sit. I am worried, Sarah. Yes, about Lizzy and the girls, but Sarah, Lizzy accused Tryphena in the presence of the Sheriff."

"Accused her of what?"

"Of having an interest in William and more than that. She accused her of having an interest in his murder."

"That's ridiculous, Father."

"Sarah, do you know of any interest between William and Tryphena?"

"What do you mean?"

"Have you known of any interactions between William and Tryphena that were..." he hesitated as if he were choking on the next words. "...that were familiar?"

"No, absolutely not! William would never do that! Never!"

"Then why would Lizzy say such a thing? It seemed so readily available for her to say. It was not as if she struggled to infer it."

Sarah's eyes narrowed. "Because she is a hateful person! I have been trying to tell you this for years, but you only thought me to be jealous of her. Do not listen to what she said about Tryphena. Do not listen to it!"

"Oh, my dear, Sarah. I wish you would have come to me. There are things you are not aware of. Things your brother had done that you know nothing about."

"What are you talking about?"

Thomas hung his head. "I am being punished by Almighty God. That is what I am talking about. I let my hatred of the Salisbury family and my greed get in the way. Now God has punished me by taking my son."

"Father, you are talking like a mad man! What do you mean?"

"Oh, Sarah, I am ashamed."

"Stop it! Father, you are scaring me! Tell me!"

"Your brother is dead because I went along with a plan that he had involving Lizzy and the property that she owned. It's a long story, dear, but after Lizzy's first husband became sick, Willie came up with the idea of going to work for her."

"That's not true. Lizzy asked him, not the other way around."

"No, no. Willie had the notion that if he helped out there, then after Nathan died, he could step up, marry Lizzy, and the property would then be his to do with as he pleased."

"I don't understand?" Sarah grabbed her father's hand and repeated, "I don't understand."

"I've always wanted that property, Sarah, for the mill. You know this. When it looked as if there was an opportunity for us to attain it, Willie decided the best way to get hold of the property was to marry the Widow Salisbury."

110

Sarah stood up and backed up slightly from the table. She was horrified at what was she just heard. "I cannot believe what I am hearing! How could you go along with such a thing? No, this cannot be true! William would have told me."

"No, Sarah, he didn't tell you. And that isn't all."

"Oh, God, Father! How could there be more? How? And you come in here and scold me that I have brought disgrace upon this family! No father, I would not say that I was the one who has done such a thing! I fear I cannot bear what you will say next!"

Thomas began to shake. "I overheard a conversation, Sarah. I dismissed the meaning of it, but I heard it."

"What was it about?"

"I heard William telling Tryphena about the property and that under the law, he could not sell it without Lizzy's permission because it belonged to her through the previous marriage."

"And?"

"And she said that Willie needed to figure out a way to get Lizzy to agree to sell it to me. He began to go on and on about how he thought at the beginning he could do this to her, but now he had realized that he loved her, and he didn't want to force her to do anything."

"That is not a bad thing," Sarah commented.

"Tryphena became angry at him. She began to accuse him of treachery against the family. I never heard her speak in such a manner. She even said something along the lines of, 'how could you do this to me – to me – Willie?"

Sarah looked at the man she called Father. He was broken and shaking visibly. She reached over and took his hand. "I understand, Papa. The accusation and your fear inside your heart, is that maybe it wasn't Lizzy?"

"I have loved her, but I fear she has never really loved me. She was the one who gave him the tonic before he died. It was not Lizzy." He began to weep.

"No! No! Papa! Lizzy was the one who purchased the arsenic, not one time, but two! Get your mind straight on that fact! It was Lizzy. I heard her talking with that John Chapman. She was saying that it didn't take this long with Nathan. She did it, Papa! It was not Tryphena! Do not talk of such a thing! And do not say a word of this idea of yours to anyone." She got up and paced back and forth briefly. "I must go out. I will be back soon."

As the door closed behind her, Tryphena came down the stairs. Seeing Thomas, she rushed towards him. "Thomas! Are you okay?"

He shook his head. "Please dear, send for the doctor. I am not feeling very well."

Chapter 10
The Missing Box

Back to modern-day – the FBI building, Indianapolis

I ask you again, Detective," Robert questioned. "Is my wife alive?"

"I don't know, Mr. Willis. I do not have confirmation from my sources one way or another."

Robert sat down and looked at the ground as if the weight of the world had just landed upon his shoulders.

"Robert? May I call you Robert?"

"Yes."

"Robert, we need your help."

"You need my help? With what?"

"I showed you the pictures that your wife sent to us. But they were just pictures. She said she had the documents, but she didn't send them here.

"So what?"

"So, surveillance shows that she did not have them with her when she entered the police station either. That means that she placed them somewhere. Do you know where she might have placed them?"

"What kind of documents?" Robert asked.

"Land transfers, wills, probate documents - have you seen anything like that?"

"No."

"Come now, think hard."

"I am not an idiot, Detective. Don't you think if I saw something like that I would know?"

"Yes, of course. And I am not implying you are an idiot."

"Why don't you just get them yourself from the courthouse?"

"We tried. Everything has been erased or edited. We need the originals."

'What do you mean they have been erased or edited? Everyone knows that anything on a computer can be recovered."

"Most of the time, that is true. But whoever erased them knew what they were doing. It's wiped clean. Your wife stumbled upon something very big, and it goes up pretty high."

"I don't follow you."

"Okay." The detective took in a deep breath. "Years ago, the Potawatomi Indians ceded the land under a treaty to the United States Government. In about eighteen hundred thirty-four, David Vanderhoof, the grandfather to William Vanderhoof, settled in the land. Eventually, the Salisbury family, also early settlers, moved in and purchased land out from under the nose of the Vanderhoof family. There was a rivalry for years between the elders in the family. After William married Elizabeth, he wanted to sell the land to his father, but she would not go along with it. And, at the time, she was the sole owner of the property. They had a great falling out. Then, allegedly, there was a plan. Although it is uncertain to this day how it was done, there was a plan to get the land registered in William's name

114

instead of just in her name. Of course, she knew nothing of this. But after he died and she went to prison, it was found that the property, which they thought they had successfully taken from her behind her back, had never been transferred. They couldn't locate the transfer document. So there was a new document made. It was not a legal one because it didn't contain her signature, but it was a document, and it gave Thomas Vanderhoof control over the property."

"So what?"

"Shortly after that, while excavating the land, they came across what looked to be an entrance to an old mine. But it turned out to be an old Indian mound, like a burial chamber, and inside were valuable items that the Indians must have confiscated during their raids and buried with that warrior. Some of the items sold for a great sum of money and over time as Indian artifacts became collectible; those were also sold. As you may have guessed, some of those items were extremely valuable. Some of them have sold in the millions of dollars to collectors. And they have made a few people very wealthy."

"The Vanderhoofs?"

"Yes, to name one of them."

"And the others?"

"Let's say that the reason nobody wants those documents to surface is that they could be challenged by the descendants and result in a multi-million dollar lawsuit. Also, should this be found out, it could bring down some people higher up who are very aware of what has transpired and have enriched themselves, too."

"So the people who were in my house are looking for those the land transfer documents because they were able to clear the

115

computers, but Lynn got those before they were able to make everything disappear?"

"Yes, I'm pretty sure they are looking for those. And so again, Mr. Willis, are you sure you do not know where they are?"

"I'm positive."

Doug scooted his foot over under the table and tapped Robert's foot. Robert didn't budge but stared straight ahead.

"I believe if we find the papers, Mr. Willis, we will have what we need to make the arrests and to find your wife ."

The woman behind the glass dialed Detective Harvey's phone. After looking at the number on the phone, he stood up said, "Gentlemen, I'm sorry, but I will need to end this discussion. Mr. Willis, my suggestion would be to stay somewhere other than your home. If someone is following you or attempting to get into your home, then you are not safe there." Reaching into his pocket, he pulled out a card. "Here. Call me if you need anything at all or especially if you come across those documents. Detective Harvey left and once again entered the room with the one-way mirror. The dark-haired woman turned around.

"He's lying. He found the documents."

"How do you know?"

"I just got a call from the diver that I put in at the other end of the lake. The box is missing."

"Why didn't you get the diver in there sooner?"

"We had to wait until we wouldn't be noticed. The lake is very busy, and others are watching."

"Detective Harvey ran his fingers thru his hair. I guess it's time to take a trip to Vandalia and search the house. Why do you think he is hiding them?"

"Plain and simple. For insurance, Detective. As long as he has them, he believes he has a chance of finding his wife."

"And what about his wife? What are we going to do about that situation? Is the plan the same?"

The dark-haired woman turned back towards the one-way mirror and watched as Robert and Doug were being escorted out of the room by Detective Marle. "That is going to be a heart-breaker, Detective Harvey. Yes, the plan is still the same."

Chapter 11
The Visitors

Nancy Hardy burst through the jailhouse doors. Her stout little body was bundled heavily to protect her from the cold. Seeing Elizabeth in the small cell, she hurried over towards her. "Lizzy! Lizzy! Is it true what I have heard?"

Sighing deeply and as if it was a great effort, Elizabeth stood up and walked over towards the bars that held her captive, and as she did, she lost her balance slightly. John jumped up to grab her.

"Hey, are you okay? Here, Lizzy. Sit down." He pushed the chair close to the bars so that she could speak with her mother.

"No, mother. Of course, it's not true. Why would you even ask such a thing?"

"I heard about it this morning. Mrs. Redding came to see me, and she told me that they held you against your will in the barn."

"Mrs. Redding is a busy-body! I bet she has this all over town by now. Have you seen the girls?"

"No, but I plan to go later to fetch them." She removed her bonnet, revealing her thinning grey hair.

"Ma'am, would you like a chair?" the voice behind her asked.

Mrs. Hardy turned toward Sheriff Clark and snapped at him. "Do not show your hypocrisy towards me, Sir! You kept my daughter, a proper lady, in a barn all night long with the likes of the three of you, and now you keep her in this cell like a caged animal! How dare you want to act as if you are a gentleman by offering a chair to me!"

"Ma'am, I can assure you that your daughter was not harmed by the other two men or me."

"Well, I will take that up with the Judge when I see him!"

"That's fine. He will be here today."

Elizabeth's attention was peaked. "Today, Sheriff? The Judge will be here today?"

"Yes, that is correct."

"Do you think he will let me go home to my girls, Sheriff?"

"I can't say."

Turning back towards her mother, she added, "Don't be so foolish, Mother. Take the chair!" Then she raised her voice just slightly so that the others in the room could hear. "I have a little morning sickness, Mother."

"Morning sickness?" Nancy scooted her chair closer and whispered, "Lizzy, are you with child?"

"You need not whisper, Mother. Yes, I am with child."

Nancy gasped. "Oh, my! What are we to do? You cannot be here in your condition."

"It seems that I have no choice right now."

"Sherriff Clarke, I demand that you release my daughter. This is no place for a woman who is expecting a child. And to think you kept her in a barn!"

"She will stay where she is until the Judge says otherwise, Ma'am."

"This is brutal, Sheriff! You can believe that I will take my complaint to the Judge!"

"Rest assured, Ma'am, if there is anything that Elizabeth needs, she will be provided with it. But until the time as the Judge determines, she will remain here."

Elizabeth sighed, "Mother, listen carefully to me. I fear I will need an attorney. Would you please fetch one for me?"

"Whom shall I go after, Lizzy?"

"I suspect you will need to go to Niles. I am thinking of Mr. Clapp & Mr. Bridgeman."

"And what shall I offer them as payment?"

"I have the means to pay. Please, ask them to come."

Just as the Sheriff turned the page on the paper he was reading, Judge Gilbert arrived. He was a heavy man with dark eyes and a black beard to match. The cold seemed to follow him through the door as he entered. Shaking the snow from his coat, he greeted Sheriff Clarke and asked if the Deputy would fetch Mr. Kellogg, the prosecutor.

Briefly, as the Judge walked towards the desk to take his seat, he looked in the cell at Lizzy and John in a judgemental sort of way. Then he busied himself looking through a few documents of cases he would listen to this month, including the one about the arrest of Lizzy and John.

"Judge Gilbert," Nancy Hardy approached him. "I think the treatment of my daughter has been horrendous! Just look at her. She is pale and weak and hasn't eaten anything in two days. And are you aware she had to spend the night in a barn like a common animal?"

"Mrs. Hardy, I am quite certain that the Sheriff made sure that no harm came to your daughter. She looks as if she is still in one piece to me, and I see no injuries about her body."

Nancy Hardy huffed as if she didn't know what to say. The judge dismissed her presence and instead turned to Sheriff Clarke. The two began having a conversation about their families and catching up as if they were good friends. Finally, James Kellogg, the prosecutor, arrived.

"Alright!" the Judge said. "First order of business - Mr. Chapman, you are free to go. I see no evidence or reason to hold you. Does the prosecutor agree?"

"Yes, I do."

Sheriff Clarke walked over to the cell and unlocked the door. "You heard him, Chapman. You are free to leave."

"And what of Lizzy?" he replied, not moving towards the open cell door.

The judge interjected, "Elizabeth, you will be held on three thousand dollars bond. The trial will commence in one week."

"Three thousand dollars! That's outrageous!" John raised his voice

"Outrageous or not, my decision stands."

John walked closer to the jail cell. "Don't worry, Lizzy. I will see the attorneys myself. They will get you out of here." She didn't say anything, but walked back over toward the old cot and sat down. Her mother continued to chatter, but she wasn't listening. She was thinking; thinking about John, about her girls, and William. But mostly she was thinking about her trial.

It was near lunchtime the next day when she was awoken from her nap by a man's voice beckoning to her. She sat up to find a nicely dressed middle-aged man of medium height and similar build. He was a handsome man, she thought, with blue eyes, blonde hair, and a sharp jawline.

"Elizabeth? Elizabeth Vanderhoof?"

"Yes, that is my name. To whom might I be speaking?"

"My name is George Bridgeman. I am with the firm Clapp and Bridgeman. It appears we have some discussion that must take place."

Trying to straighten her dress and smooth her hair, she said, "It appears we do. I apologize that my appearance is less than acceptable. It is hard to keep one's self up in such a place as this."

The attorney ignored her comment and instead turned to the Sheriff. "Sir, I require a private audience with Mrs. Vanderhoof. I will need you to leave, or I will need to be provided with another location in which Mrs. Vanderhoof and I can speak privately."

Stretching his arms out on each side of his body, Sheriff Clarke stood. "I guess I will let you both talk in here. I'll go across the road and get a cup of fresh coffee. You have an hour."

As Sheriff Clarke left the building, Mr. Bridgeman pulled up a chair and sat down. Elizabeth began by saying, "I would like to know if...". The attorney put up his hand as if to silence her. Then he said, "Mrs. Vanderhoof, I have one question right now, just one. And I want you to think very carefully before you answer it. Did you or did you not poison your husband?"

"I did no such thing!"

"Mrs. Vanderhoof, I am going to ask you again. Did you or did you not poison your husband?"

"This is preposterous! I just answered that question. And the answer is still no."

"There seems to be a preponderance of evidence against you, my dear, suggesting that you did, in fact, poison your husband."

"And what evidence would that be, Sir?"

"Evidence that shows you purchased the very poison found in Mr. Vanderhoof's body. Do you deny purchasing such a poison?"

"I do not deny it. I purchased it because we had rats about the house. Dr. Mann was tending to my husband in our home and instructed me to get Rough on Rats, but the druggist had none, and so I requested strychnine, but the druggist did not have any strychnine either. It was the druggist himself who suggested arsenic."

"I see. And what would you say to the fact that another receipt was discovered?. One in which you purchased arsenic while you were married to your first husband."

"I would say it is a lie and a forgery. I never did any such thing."

"Mrs. Vanderhoof, would you have me to believe that the druggist made that up?"

"Mr. Bridgeman, whose employ are you in? Did you come here to defend me, or did you come here to get information to help the prosecution?"

"If you could just answer the question, please."

"I will do no such thing! How dare you come in here and accuse me !"

Again, Mr. Bridgeman put up his hand and said, "We will need to work on that temper of yours. Do you think for one such moment that the prosecution will not ask those questions or come at you in such a manner? Well, my dear Mrs. Vanderhoof, he will do as I have done, and he will do it in front of a jury. Now, whether or not you killed or didn't kill your husband, the first and foremost thing is to make the jury believe you have been unjustly accused. A temper like that will only prove to them that you are defensive and therefore, must have committed the crime."

Elizabeth sat back, and a sly smile came to her face. "Very well done, Sir. Yes, very well done, indeed."

"Now, Mrs. Vanderhoof, let's talk about those receipts from the druggist, shall we?"

Just then the two were interrupted by Thomas and Sarah Vanderhoof who came into the small office.

"Pardon me," Mr. Bridgeman addressed them. "If you do not mind, I am in the middle of a private conversation with my client. We will be done here shortly. Please, kindly wait across the road at the diner."

"I have no idea who you are, Sir," Sarah stated. "But we will not be pushed about by the likes of you! We have come here to talk with Elizabeth, and that is what we propose to do!"

"Madam, you are intruding on a private conversation. Unless you would like me to call the Sheriff back to have you forcibly removed, I suggest you heed my advice."

"How dare you! Who do you think you are?"

"I am an officer of the court, and I am with my client. This is our private allotted time. Now, I will ask you one more time before I retrieve the Sheriff."

"Come, Sarah," Thomas instructed. "We will wait." He grabbed Sarah's arm, and the pair walked back out the same way in which they had come.

Elizabeth looked at the attorney, "Bravo! Mr. Bridgeman. Bravo! I think we are going to get along just fine."

"Mrs. Vanderhoof, whether we get along or don't get along, matters not to me. My job is to defend you, and that exactly is what I am going to do to the best of my intellect. I dare say that I do not like to play games. I expect honesty, total honesty, whether it be good or bad, and we deal with it between us. I cannot represent someone without knowing all the facts. Now, let's talk about that first receipt of arsenic. Did you or did you not purchase arsenic in eighteen hundred seventy-six while you were married to Nathan Salisbury?"

She sat back on the chair and stared at the man in front of her. Her eyes began to narrow, and then the sly smile that he had seen from her earlier came back to her face. "Yes, Mr. Bridgeman. I was with Mr. Vanderhoof several years ago when we purchased arsenic."

"I am afraid you do not understand my question. I asked if you purchased arsenic when you were married to Nathan Salisbury. In your reply, you stated you were with Mr. Vanderhoof."

"That is correct. I was married to Nathan Salisbury, and William Vanderhoof was a hired man for Mr. Salisbury and myself. We had gone into town for supplies. Nathan was not able to go as he was bed-bound. While in town, Mr. Vanderhoof stated that we had rats in the barn, which is where he was sleeping, and he asked me to purchase some arsenic along with some tooth powder. I gave the arsenic to Mr. Vanderhoof, and I kept the tooth powder."

"Why did you lie to me earlier when I asked about the arsenic?"

"There were rumors when Nathan died. Crazy rumors that he had been poisoned. My mind went immediately to the arsenic that I had gotten for Willie. I didn't want you to think bad of Willie."

"What are you saying? Are you saying William Vanderhoof poisoned your first husband?"

"I am saying that I purchased arsenic for William at his request due to the rats in the barn where he was keeping quarters. And that is what I will say in court if I am questioned regarding it. I will say no more and no less."

"And so you defer the implication in the rumors of the murder of your first husband to your second husband, who cannot either confirm nor deny your allegations?"

She stood up and stretched. "I believe I have just handed you a portion of your defense strategy, Mr. Bridgeman." At that exact moment, Sheriff Clarke walked back in followed by Thomas and Sarah Vanderhoof.

"Time's up, Mr. Bridgeman," the Sheriff replied. "These folks have something they would like to speak to Mrs. Vanderhoof about."

Before George Bridgeman could reply, Elizabeth interjected, "Mr. Bridgeman, I would like you to remain and bear witness as to this conversation."

"Lizzy, this is between you and us," Thomas stated.

"You heard my request, Thomas. Anything you would like to say to me can be said in the presence of my legal representative."

"Oh, this is nonsense!" Sarah spoke up and stepped forward. "Elizabeth, you have a stallion that was given to William from my father. We are just informing you that we will be retrieving the stallion."

"You will do no such thing!" George Bridgeman said. "You will not so much as remove a blade of grass from my client's property without her consent. To do anything else will be considered trespassing and theft. Just because she is here does not give you authority to take her possessions. And let us all be clear. That horse is her possession as passed on through the death of her husband."

"That horse was a gift to my son, William, out of my private inventory," Thomas said. "I find with the charges leveled against Elizabeth towards my son, that it is appropriate to retrieve the horse."

"Mr. Vanderhoof, Elizabeth is innocent until proven guilty. You will stay off of her property and away from that horse, and might I add, if the horse turns up missing you will be held responsible. I am certain I make myself clear."

Thomas bristled, and Sarah took his arm. "Come, father." She looked at Elizabeth and snapped, "You may think you won, Lizzy but you won't win in the end. I will see you go to prison for what you did to my brother!"

Chapter 12
The Trial Begins

The courtroom filled quickly on the morning of the trial. It mattered not that it was winter and the trails were laden with freshly fallen snow. This was the biggest thing to happen in the little town of Galien, and it seemed that in addition to over eighty witnesses that were supposed to testify, that the entire county had turned out; men as well as women. The chatter was almost deafening as the crowd waited for the court session to begin.

In the front row sat Thomas Vanderhoof. His countenance was solemn, and from the sunken appearance of his cheekbones, it looked as if he had aged ten years since his son had died. He said not a word but stared straight ahead, periodically rubbing his hands for warmth. Next to him was Tryphena, looking as nervous and uneasy as her husband. Her blond hair was pulled into a neat bun, and she too, sat stoically with her hands folded perfectly on her lap. Sitting next to her was Sarah, who had chosen a dark green bonnet for the occasion to compliment her reddish hair. She did not appear uneasy at all. She had the appearance similar to a cat who had cornered a mouse and was ready to pounce upon it.

Then, as if in a parade-like fashion, the all-male jury began to enter. Each man was dressed in his Sunday best and clean-shaven. Among the men was Henry Sheeley, one of the childhood friends of William Vanderhoof. Henry was a hardy man with curly blond hair and a reddish-blonde beard. Then there was Charles Vinton, William's neighbor who had worked side by side with him clearing the east twenty acres of land they shared between them. And then there was Bishop Jamison, a close friend of Thomas Vanderhoof. Each man took his seat in the jury box. The crowd began to settle down as they stared at the men who had been chosen to determine the fate of the accused.

Next, Elizabeth Vanderhoof entered the room with her attorney and the Sheriff by her side. A sudden hush fell over the group as every eye turned to look at her. She was clean and well-groomed. She didn't look at the group who were all their to judge her actions, but stared straight ahead and walked confidently. Whispers could be heard as she passed the crowd and took her seat at the table next to the attorney. A female voice from somewhere in the back shouted, "Murderer!" But Elizabeth didn't flinch. Then the Judge entered the room, but the murmuring continued paying no attention to his presence.

"Order in the court!" he said, slamming the gavel down upon the wooden desk. "This is the trial of the State of Michigan versus Elizabeth Vanderhoof. Is the defendant in the courtroom?"

"She is, Your Honor," Mr. Bridgeman quickly replied.

"Elizabeth Vanderhoof, please stand." As she obeyed, he continued, "Elizabeth Vanderhoof, you are present today because you are charged with the murder of your husband, William Vanderhoof, by poisoning him with arsenic. Do you understand the charges before you this day?"

"Yes, I do."

"And how do you plead?"

"I am not guilty."

"Very well, Mrs. Vanderhoof. You may take your seat. Is the prosecution ready?"

"The prosecution is ready, Your Honor," Mr. Kellogg said.

"And the defense? Is the defense ready?"

"The defense is ready, Your Honor."

"Then let us begin. Mr. Kellogg, you have the floor."

"The prosecution calls its first witness, Captain Sterns, to the stand."

The druggist, who had been sitting near the back of the room, slowly made his way through the crowd toward the front. His hair was greased flat against his head and neatly parted down the center. He had chosen a bow tie to complement a crisp white shirt for his appearance. Nervously, he passed the table at which the accused sat. He glanced in Lizzy's direction and then looked away before she would have the chance to look at him. But she was sitting like a statue and staring straight ahead, paying him no extra attention.

"Please, have a seat, Captain Sterns," the Judge directed. "Raise your right hand and place your other hand on the Bible, please. Do you swear that the information which you are about to give is the truth, the complete truth, and nothing but the truth, so help you God?"

"I..I do."

"Mr. Kellogg, you are free to begin questioning the witness."

The prosecutor wasted no time but jumped in eagerly. "Captain Sterns, it is your testimony that Mrs. Vanderhoof came to you, not once, but twice since you have known her to purchase arsenic. Correct?"

The druggist cleared his throat. "That is my testimony."

"And can you tell this court the events that surrounded those purchases?"

"Yes. Mrs. Vanderhoof came into my store last summer. She stated she was looking for something to kill rats. I told her that we had Rough on Rats, but she did not want that. She stated that her husband specifically told her to buy arsenic. I was hesitant about getting the arsenic, and so I suggested strychnine. But she again stated that Mr. Vanderhoof specifically wanted the arsenic. So, I retrieved it and told her how to mix it for the rats. Then I handed it to her but forgot to mark the package, so I took it back and marked it. I then joked with her not to commit suicide with that. She stated that if she did, I would certainly hear about it."

"And what of the other time, Mr. Sterns?"

"After Mr. Vanderhoof died, I was at home and remembered the conversation I had with Mrs. Vanderhoof this past summer. Something bothered me all night about that conversation, and then I remembered her coming into the shop many years earlier and purchasing arsenic. I couldn't remember the year, and so I took a trip to the cemetery to see the date upon Mr. Nathan Salisbury's grave. Then I hurried back to the shop and went through all my books and finally came across the journal entry in eighteen hundred seventy-six, the year in which Mr. Salisbury died. That was the year in which she purchased arsenic also."

"Thank you, Captain Sterns."

Mr. Bridgeman stood up and walked slowly over towards the Captain. "Mr. Sterns, is it not true that you have what one would call an infatuation with Miss Sarah Vanderhoof?" A gasp was heard from the front row of the crowd where Sarah was sitting.

"Objection!" Mr. Kellogg called out.

The Judge spoke, "What is the relevancy of the question, Mr. Bridgeman?"

"The relevancy is the motive for the information provided to Miss Sarah Vanderhoof, Your Honor."

"The objection is overruled. You may proceed."

Turning back towards the witness, the attorney once again spoke, "Mr. Sterns, is it true that you have an infatuation with Miss Sarah Vanderhoof?"

He looked over at Sarah momentarily and then looked down and did not answer the question.

"Come now, Captain. This is a court of law. Surely there are those in this courtroom that could testify to this truth if you do not. And so I ask you again, Sir."

"Yes, it is true that I find Miss Vanderhoof, ...that I fancy her, yes."

"Would you say, Sir, that you would like her to fancy you, as well?"

Captain Sterns hung his head and fiddled with his fingers.

"Again, my good man, you have taken an oath to speak the truth."

He looked up at the attorney with an annoyed look on his face. "Yes, I fancy Miss Vanderhoof, and yes, I would like it if she thought the same of me. What is your point besides embarrassment for myself and Miss Vanderhoof?"

"My point is that you found this evidence, or so-called evidence, and didn't go to the Sheriff or Mr. Thomas Vanderhoof, or even the Prosecutor. You went direct to Miss Sarah Vanderhoof. You went to her to impress her so that she would fancy you as you say. Isn't that true, Mr. Sterns?"

133

"I went to her because she is the sister of the deceased."

"No, Mr. Sterns. You went to her specifically and not to the Sheriff, nor Mr. Vanderhoof, nor the prosecutor. Dare I say you wanted her to think you a hero of sorts?"

"That is ridiculous!"

"Is it? Is it ridiculous that any other person would have gone to the proper authorities, and yet you go to Miss Vanderhoof? Dare I say that you tried to impress her, knowing her dislike for the accused, Elizabeth Vanderhoof. And you figured that if you provided information to Miss Sarah Vanderhoof that would implicate her sister-in-law, her enemy, that you would then become the hero and possibly win her attention? And dare I say further that you made up the entry from eighteen hundred seventy-six to give Sarah Vanderhoof fuel against her sister-in-law, whom you knew she disliked so?"

"Objection! Mr. Sterns is not on trial here, and this badgering of the witness is not acceptable!"

"Overruled! Answer the question, Captain Sterns," Judge Gilbert ordered.

"I do not know what the question is."

"The question is, Captain Sterns, did you make up the receipt to gain the attention and affection of the sister of the deceased?"

"I did no such thing!"

"Then why did you go to her instead of the authorities with the information? Why, Sir? And remember you swore an oath just moments ago."

The druggist looked over at Sarah. "I'm sorry, Sarah. I went to Miss Vanderhoof because her mother-in-law, Tryphena, asked me to." An enormous roar came over the courtroom. Thomas

134

stood up, causing his hat to fall from his lap and said, "How dare you!"

"Order! Order in the court! If those who are not witnesses cannot control their outbursts, they will be escorted from this court! Now, Mr. Sterns, please explain your last statement."

The druggist drew in a deep breath. "The truth is, Sir, that I did go to the home of Mr. Thomas Vanderhoof. He was not at home, but his wife, Tryphena, was. She sensed the urgency of my visit, and I told her of my finding. She asked me to spare Thomas the difficulty since he had been devastated by the death of his son and asked me to speak with Sarah instead. That is what I did."

"So you went to the home of the person whom you had an interest in, namely Sarah Vanderhoof, hoping to show information against Mrs. Elizabeth Vanderhoof, to gain favor within the family."

"No! No! That is not how it was!"

"Wasn't it, Mr. Sterns?"

"Objection!"

"What are your grounds for objection, Mr. Kellogg," the judge questioned.

"Speculation, Your Honor."

"Objection sustained. Mr. Bridgeman, please contain your arguments to facts."

"I am finished with the witness," he responded and took his seat next to Lizzy.

Mr. Kellogg stood up and postured himself as if he were about to give a speech. "The prosecution calls Dr. Levi Mann."

Dr. Mann stood up, straightened his brown suit coat, and headed towards the front of the room. After taking the oath, he sat down, stroked his white beard in an almost nervous fashion, and then folded his hands on his lap.

"Dr. Mann, can you tell me how you came to know Mr. William Vanderhoof?"

"Yes. Mr. Vanderhoof came to see me about three years ago complaining of heart pain and stomach ailments."

"And what was your conclusion as to his condition, and what was your treatment of such?"

"Well, Mr. Vanderhoof's condition was perplexing. He complained of stomach pain after eating, yet he also complained of being short of breath and dizzy. I wasn't sure at the time what his condition really was. So I began to treat him for a stomach condition. I prescribed a tonic to be taken before meals."

"And did this tonic offer him any relief?"

"It didn't seem to. His condition began to deteriorate, and last summer, he took a sharp decline. I could come up with no logical, medical explanation for his condition and his symptoms. It all makes sense now."

"What makes sense, Doctor?"

"That Mr. Vanderhoof was poisoned. The symptoms all show the poisoning."

"How so, Doctor?"

"His symptoms the night leading up to his death are synonymous with arsenic poisoning. I believe that Mr. Vanderhoof had been given a fatal dose of arsenic the night of his death. Tapping his fingers on the book he had brought to the stand with him, he said, "In fact, according to this medical journal it describes the symptoms of arsenic poisoning, which are the exact symptoms Mr. Vanderhoof had."

"And so it is your professional opinion that Mr. Vanderhoof was administered arsenic the night of his death and that is what led to his death?"

"Yes. That is my professional opinion."

"And could arsenic in common medicinal tinctures have caused this?"

"No, it could not have."

"So, you believe without a doubt that the death of Mr. William Vanderhoof was that of an intentional poisoning?"

"I certainly do."

"Thank you, Doctor."

Mr. Bridgeman stood up and tugged on his vest. He walked casually up to the witness and tapped on the witness stand as if he were thinking. "Dr. Mann, you said Mr. Vanderhoof was very ill. And how long had you treated him again?"

"Three years."

"Three years? And during those three years what were you treating him for?"

"Stomach complaint."

"Stomach complaint? And what of the heart complaint, Doctor?"

"I didn't treat him for a heart complaint."

"Why, Sir? You state in your testimony that Mr. Vanderhoof himself complained of heart issue, yet you did not treat him for such?"

"I believed his trouble to be stomach related."

"I see. And tell me, did you spend a great deal of time at the Vanderhoof home?"

"Yes. Yes, I did."

"And isn't it true you would show up at the Vanderhoof residence uninvited to check on Mr. Vanderhoof?"

"It is my job to check on my patients."

"Were you called upon Sir, or did you take it upon yourself to see Mr. Vanderhoof regardless of the invitation?"

"I did go see Mr. Vanderhoof often. I was worried about him."

"Worried about him? And while you were there worrying about him, did you witness anything unusual in the behavior of Mrs. Vanderhoof toward her husband?"

"No."

"Did you ever notice her being unkind to him or not caring for him?"

"No, I can't say that to be true."

"Didn't you compliment Mrs. Vanderhoof on what a good and doting wife she was?"

"Yes, I believe I said that to her at one point."

"Didn't you also tell her at one point when Mr. Vanderhoof was bedridden that you would always be available for her if anything were to happen to him?"

"You make that sound devious, Mr. Bridgeman. I was inferring that I would be available to come should his condition deteriorate."

"Really, Doctor? Then the fact that Mrs. Vanderhoof had to ask you to leave for being inappropriate with her is not true?"

"I do not know what you are talking about?"

"Don't you? Isn't it true that you made an unwelcome advance toward Mrs. Vanderhoof, and when she told you that it wasn't welcome that you became upset, and she had to ask you to leave?"

138

"No."

"Isn't it true, Doctor, that this wasn't the first unwelcome advance that you had made towards Mrs. Vanderhoof and the very next visit you changed the tonic to a power for Mrs. Vanderhoof to mix for her husband?"

"I did change his medicine upon the request of my colleague, Dr. Henderson. The previous one was not working."

"And the new medicine, did it contain arsenic?"

"Preposterous!"

"Preposterous? Why preposterous, Doctor?"

"Are you implying that I gave the arsenic to William Vanderhoof that caused his death?"

"I didn't say that, Doctor. I asked if the new medicine contained arsenic. Medicines do contain some arsenic at times. Do they not? It was only you, Doctor, who drew another conclusion. I find that interesting. I also find it interesting that you have never suspected poisoning even once during the three years that you treated Mr. Vanderhoof. But now you suddenly say it is all clear, and it must have been poisoning. Tell me, Doctor. How could it be then that you were treating Mr. Vanderhoof for heart trouble and stomach trouble? Yet, here today, you state he had all the symptoms of arsenic poisoning; a condition that you did not notice or think to be the cause until it was suggested by the prosecution?"

"I did not know what was wrong with Mr. Vanderhoof. His symptoms perplexed me."

"Yet, you state that you never considered poisoning, which indicates that you, Doctor Mann, did not suspect poisoning. You also did not consult this medical journal which you bring with you today that had the very symptoms of arsenic poisoning

139

within its pages. So either you truly did not suspect Mr. Vanderhoof to be the victim of poisoning, or you are incompetent at your trade. Which is it?"

Doctor Mann stood up. "I will not allow you to ruin my good name!"

"Dear Sir, I am not attempting to ruin your good name any more than you are attempting to ruin the good name of Mrs. Elizabeth Vanderhoof. I have no further questions for you, Doctor Mann." The Doctor stood up, snatched the book, and walked out of the courthouse.

"The prosecution next calls Dr. Henderson."

Dr. Henderson was a thin, frail man with white hair. He took his time getting to the witness seat.

"Doctor, how long have you been practicing medicine?"

"I have been a physician for thirty years."

"And how did you come to know Mr. Vanderhoof, the deceased?"

"I was contacted by Dr.Mann."

"Oh? And why was that?"

"He had stated that Mr. William Vanderhoof had puzzling symptoms, and he could not determine what was wrong with him. He asked if I might consider taking a look at him to see if I could help."

"And what were your findings, Doctor?"

"After examination of Mr. Vanderhoof, I did not understand what his trouble was. His heart rate was slightly elevated, but I attributed that to nervousness. He had a nervousness about him. I think this because he was fidgeting with his hands and his legs were in motion also. His gaze was almost wild-like, continually looking about the room. He stated that he would eat and then shortly after eating, he would feel as if he couldn't breathe, and his stomach would begin to hurt him. He also looked emaciated."

"And did you think it was heart trouble?"

"No, I did not think it to be heart trouble."

"And what did you think it to be?"

"At that time, I believed he was suffering from stomach ailments. I told Mr. Vanderhoof that I wanted to give him a powder with some quinine and calomel. He was not enthusiastic about that because he stated if it would not help him, then he would rather take nothing at all. I assured him, he would do better attempting a cure than none at all."

"And what happened next?"

"I spoke with Dr. Mann, who agreed that a new powder should be given. And Dr. Mann mixed up the powder and brought it out to the Vanderhoof residence that evening."

"And to whom did he give the powder and the dosing instructions?"

"It was given to Mrs. Vanderhoof."

"So, the powder was something that had to be mixed, and he gave the mixing instructions to Mrs. Vanderhoof as well?"

"Yes, that is correct."

"And have you had the opportunity to examine the findings from the autopsy, Doctor?"

"Yes, I have read those."

"And what is your opinion of those?"

"After reading those and reviewing my notes regarding Mr. Vanderhoof's symptoms, I believe his death was caused by poisoning."

"Thank you, Doctor. "

The defense attorney quickly walked up to the witness. "Dr. Henderson, you stated that you instructed Dr. Mann to mix up Calomel and Quinine. Why Calomel Dr.?"

"Calomel was for his bowels to help loosen them."

"And the Quinine?"

"It was for worms."

"Worms? So you believed Mr. Vanderhoof had worms that were causing his troubles?"

"I wasn't sure, but I believed this to be the best course of treatment."

"Doctor, I assume in your medical studies that you also studied tinctures and their effects against disease, did you not?"

"I did."

"And I did as well. Before becoming an attorney, I also studied to become a physician. I, too, am well acquainted with these mixtures – this quinine and calomel. And for a man suffering from intense stomach pain, you chose these two mixtures? Two mixtures that would heavily burden his intestines more than they already were? Two mixtures that if taken in the wrong quantity can produce fatal results? These are the mixtures you chose?"

"I beg your pardon, Mr. Bridgeman! I am a doctor of medicine, and I choose what will benefit my patient the most. I chose those medicines for their benefit of Mr. Vanderhoof's ailments."

"But you had no knowledge of Mr. Vanderhoof having worms, yet you chose Quinine? And you chose Calomel to produce bowel movements, which it does in great quantities, yet you stated Mr. Vanderhoof was already emaciated. Are you aware, Doctor, that Mr. Vanderhoof's health rapidly declined after he began taking this new mixture?"

Dr. Henderson drew in his breath and held what everyone could tell was a temper outburst. "His health was in decline even before I changed the medication."

"Ahhh, so you acknowledge that his health was in decline, something you would have had to been told because you, Doctor, stated that you had been called for a consultation. You would not have been aware of the decline in his health as you were not his attending physician. Is this correct?"

"It is correct that I was summoned for a consultation, and Doctor Mann told me that Mr. Vanderhoof's health had been declining, and he didn't know the reason."

"So, Dr. Henderson, by your admission, Dr. Mann told you of Mr. Vanderhoof's declining health, and this would then imply that Dr. Mann also acknowledged that Mr. Vanderhoof was declining in health and that Mr. Vanderhoof had a chronic condition and not an acute one. You further testified that Mr. Vanderhoof had mysterious symptoms. He did not have common constipation and worms. These common symptoms Dr. Mann himself would have been able to diagnosis. He would not have needed your opinion for those symptoms. Yet, you prescribed medication to treat common symptoms. And furthermore, Dr. Mann himself stated that Mr. Vanderhoof's condition worsened after he began taking this new tincture. Why do you suppose that is?"

"Mr. Vanderhoof's symptoms worsened because he was being poisoned."

"But Doctor, neither you nor Dr. Mann suspected poisoning. You both treated for a chronic condition. Neither you nor Dr.

Mann believed it to be poisoning. Neither of you consulted the Medical Journal, and if you did, you still did not believe it to be poisoning. Yet you come here today and swear under oath that it was poisoning. So I will put to you the same question as was put to Dr. Mann. Either you didn't believe Mr. Vanderhoof was being poisoned or you are incompetent in your field. Which is it?"

"Now, wait just a minute," the doctor stood to object. "Do not insult me!"

"No further questions, Your Honor," Mr. Bridgeman said.

"Doctor, you have been dismissed. The court will take a break for lunch. Please return at one o'clock."

Chapter 13
Robert Returns Home

Robert and Doug left the city of Indianapolis as quickly as they had arrived. They did not notice the dark blue vehicle behind them that was watching their every move.

"Oh, man," Doug said. "What do you think that was all about, and why did you tell them you didn't know where the documents were?"

"I don't know, and I'm not sure we can trust any one of them or anything they say. Something tells me we need to hold on to those papers. They were important enough for Lynn to hide them."

"Okay, Dude, let's just go through this from the beginning and maybe we can figure out what our next move is."

Robert nodded his head in agreement. "Okay, okay. So, Lynn finds these diaries years ago and doesn't get around to reading them until just recently. Then she notices something about a trial."

"Right! That's a good point. Maybe we should look for information on that."

"Maybe. Then as she starts to research it and she finds out about the murder or so-called murder and begins asking questions around in Galien. It was about then that she began to tell me that she thought she was being followed."

"Did you ever see anyone following her or hanging around the house?"

"No. I thought it was odd. I mean, think about where we live; down a hill across from a lake. Nobody comes in or out without the neighbors knowing. That is why I had a hard time believing her."

"Maybe nobody was following her. Maybe it was just her imagination."

"She's gone, Doug. Is that her imagination?"

"Maybe she wanted you to think that."

"What?"

"Just follow my thinking for a minute, Dude. Don't you find it weird that the police have not questioned you at all in her disappearance? Don't you think it is weird that the FBI didn't question you? It's like they know that you are not guilty. How could they know that? Maybe they know what happened, and you are being used as a pawn."

Robert pulled over to the side of the road and stared in his rearview mirror as a blue car sped on past him.

"What's up?" Doug asked.

"I'm pretty sure we were being followed."

"Followed? By who?"

"Really, Doug? Are you really asking that question? Do you think I would know the answer to that?" He pulled back onto the road and quickly took the nearest exit into a little town, and then pulled into a gas station. He motioned for Doug to get out of the vehicle with him. "We need to search inside the vehicle. I think someone has been in here."

"What? How do you know?"

"I think those guys at the FBI, but I'm not sure. I know we were being followed, and I want to be sure that they can't locate us right now. So start looking quickly." After a minute, Robert said, "Hey, the vape battery is different. Only someone who knows that I vape would know that I have this charger in my vehicle. Remember, they searched us when we got there. They had my vaporizer. They could have been in here while we were in there. And it's no coincidence that I noticed a dark car behind us for miles, and it continued to follow every move I was making. And, come to think of it, you are right, Doug. Why haven't they questioned me about my wife? That should have been the first thing they would have done. Something isn't right. Why was he so insistent that I don't go home?" He reached over the console in the vehicle and disconnected the vape battery charger and threw it into the trash can at the gas station. I need to think! Let's stop as soon as we find a little place where we can get a bite to eat, and then I am going home!"

It was getting late, and they were just about ten minutes from his house when his phone buzzed. It was his neighbor, Scott.

"Scott? What's up?"

"Robert, thank God you are alright! Where are you? What's going on? There are FBI agents at your house!"

"What! What do you mean?"

"I mean that they just arrived about five minutes ago, and they are in the house. One just went down by your boat!"

Robert didn't say anything but hung up the phone. He pressed on the gas peddle and soon was near the top of the hill that led down to his home. Quietly, he pulled into the woods and jumped out.

"Robert! Where are you going?"

"Shh!" He made his way across his neighbor's property and towards the back of his house. Slowly, he approached the house and looked around. Then he peeked into a window. There were two agents in his bedroom. One was male, and one was a female. Both of them had on FBI jackets, and both were going through items in the room. The male turned around, and Robert recognized detective Webster from the Vandalia police station. The woman's back was still facing him. He wasn't sure who she was, but she had dark hair pulled into a ponytail. Finally, after several minutes, she turned around. Robert gasped.

Doug gasped along with him, "Oh, my God! What the hell?"

But Robert was already moving towards the back door. One of the agents in the driveway heard movement and was heading towards the back, but it was too late. Robert had already gotten into the house and to the back room, where he confronted the agents. Both of the agents looked up. And then Lynn realized what Robert had found out.

"Oh, my God! What the hell is going on here? Lynn! My God! Lynn! What the hell is happening?"

Two of the agents grabbed him, throwing him up against the wall. "No, let him go," she instructed. "He's okay." He was quickly frisked and then released. "Robert, honey, listen to me."

"Listen to you? Listen to you! How about you tell me what the hell is going on?"

"Robert, calm down. Take a deep breath."

"Take a deep breath? For Christ's sake, Lynn! I thought you were dead! I have been going through hell wondering what has happened to you and you have been fine all along? Are you an FBI agent? Oh, my God! What the ...."

"Jake," she said to the other agent in the room with her. "Please leave us alone for a few moments."

Once he had left, Robert fell to his knees and back against the wall. "What the hell is going on, Lynn?"

She squatted in front of him, "Robert, listen to me. I can explain all of this to you."

"Can you? Can you explain how you disappeared and put your husband through hell? Can you explain why you would leave someone wondering if you are alive or dead? Can you explain what you are doing in my house with these men? Please, tell me this is a bad dream!"

"Robert, please, calm down," she said as she reached for his arm.

"Calm down? Calm down! Do you think I should calm down? I will calm down when I know just what the hell is going on!" He moved his arm away from her grasp.

She leaned back against the wall. "Okay, this isn't going to be easy. But I guess I owe you the truth."

"You think?" he said sarcastically.

"The truth is that I am an FBI agent. I always have been. I have been with the FBI since I left college."

"How could you? You were married and had kids. You moved to a farm. You told me that."

"I did get married, and I did have kids. Yes, that is all true. But I was still working for the FBI at that time. The marriage was necessary as a cover and because my identity had been compromised at that time."

"What? What kind of a person are you? You married someone to hide, not because you loved him?"

149

"Robert, listen. Please, just listen. We have been trying to break this corruption case for several years up here. I needed to be closer and...."

"And we met online!. Is that why you contacted me? Not because I had a nice smile as you wrote to me, but because you needed a cover?"

She hung her head as tears began to swell in his eyes. "Okay, yes, Robert. You were chosen because of your location. You were supposed to be the perfect cover because you were a single guy who lives in the right area and didn't have children. I was supposed to be in and out. But that isn't what happened."

"Wait a minute! Back up. Were you going to use me? I can't believe how worried I have been about you! You never once thought about me, did you?

"Please don't rush to judgment. The truth is the corruption was so deep that I was not sure who I could trust. I knew I could trust you after we met, and that is why I chose you."

"Lucky me!"

"I knew if I got into trouble that it could cost me my life. And I also knew if I gave you clues, like with the documents, you would figure them out and protect them for me. I knew you would be smart enough to do that."

"Don't flatter me! It doesn't make this any better! So all those Who Done It suppers we went to and all the games you liked to play to get me to find something, that was all for this?

She let out a heavy sigh. "Yes, it was staged. We needed to know who on the police force were dirty, and who was working for who. I had to stage my arrest to flush them out and make the others think I was out of the way. Detective Webster was also an undercover agent. So at the police station when he had me taken out through the back door, my team was waiting there to make the arrests. We knew that there were more people involved, and so we waited and watched. Once we saw Michelle, she was the blonde police officer that passed herself off as Maggie Martin, come to your house, we knew we had her.

"And the guys down in Indy? Are they in on this too?"

Her shoulders drooped even more. "Yes, and I was there also. I was watching you while you were speaking to Detective Harvey."

"How?"

"Thru the mirror."

"Oh, my God! I don't even know who you are. I mean literally, I don't know who the hell you are! Here I think I am married to a sweet, loving, caring wife, and you are nothing but a liar and a game player! Why didn't you take your stupid documents and leave? Why did you play this game? Why did you put me through this?"

"I didn't know who I could trust, Robert. I didn't know who was following me, and I didn't want to be caught with them. So I hid them, intending to come back for them. But once I realized this was much bigger than I thought, I couldn't come back. I needed you."

"So the video that I saw at Scott's house the day you disappeared, what were you doing?"

"I was writing the note and putting it in the dog bin. I knew you would look there."

"And what if I didn't?"

"There were other clues in the house. I put them there. You would have eventually figured it out, and I knew you would get the papers. So, Robert, please, I need the papers. Can you please tell me where they are?"

"So you used me to protect yourself? What about protecting me?"

"You were always protected. I always knew where you were, and there was always someone watching you."

"And our marriage, Lynn? Was it real or was that just a convenience for you also?"

She didn't answer immediately.

"Answer me! Was it just a convenience?"

"Robert, I do love you. I wasn't supposed to fall in love with you, but I do love you! Please believe at least that much."

In a softened voice, she replied, "You were chosen because of your location to what was needed. You were originally a cover, yes. But I fell in love with you. I really do love you!"

"Your disappearance? Were you going to let me believe you died, and that would be it? You were never going to come back?"

"Robert, please don't do this."

"So I'm right. That is what you were going to do and then move on to the next case or whatever the hell this is." He stood up. "You don't do this to someone you love." He turned to walk away.

"Robert, the papers, where are the papers?"

He wiped the tears from his eyes. "I don't have any papers."

"What do you mean? You took them from the garden and the box. I sent the diver in the lake at night. The box is gone."

He shook his head and lied, "Well, I don't know what box you are talking about. The only papers I had were from the garden, and I burned those after I read them." He walked toward the door and then turned one last time, "Am I in danger?"

"No," she said softly, "If you don't have the papers, then they got what they were looking for. Robert, we can work this out."

"There is nothing to work out," he said, walking out of the room and motioning for Doug who was sitting on the couch being watched by another agent. "Let's go."

Chapter 14
The Trial Continues

1884, Galien Michigan, Courthouse

The next witness that the prosecution would like to call is Professor Prescott."

Professor Prescott was a chubby, middle-aged, red-haired man with a large bushy mustache. He wore a plain black suit with a white bow tie. His voice was deep and gruff as he took the oath and promised to tell the truth. As he sat down, he looked smugly over at Elizabeth Vanderhoof who returned the gaze in the same manner.

"Professor Prescott, can you please tell me how you came to be acquainted with William Vanderhoof?"

"I was enlisted by the coroner of this county to examine the organs that were sent to me; particularly half the brain, a lobe of the lung, the heart, kidney, and stomach."

"And what were you to examine them for?"

"For the presence of arsenic."

"And would you please tell the court what it was you found?"

"In the stomach, I found nearly a half-grain of arsenious acid, otherwise known as white arsenic. In the liver, I found nine-tenths grain and slight traces of it in the kidney as well."

The prosecutor picked up one of several glass vials and brought it to the Professor. "Would you tell the court what this is?"

"This is the arsenic that I discovered inside Mr. Vanderhoof's body."

"And what was your conclusion about this matter?"

"My conclusion was that this poison was sufficient in such quantity as to have caused death, and it was in such quantity that it could not have resulted from the administration of arsenic in proper medical treatment."

"So, in your medical opinion, you believe that Mr. Vanderhoof ingested this poison that contributed to his death?"

"That is my opinion."

"Thank you, Professor."

Attorney Bridgeman stood up but did not walk over towards the Professor. "Mr. Prescott, what is your profession, Sir?"

"I am the Professor of Chemistry at the State University at Ann Arbor."

"And you state in your testimony that you examined the organs of Mr. William Vanderhoof, is that correct?"

"That is correct."

"And you state that you were employed to search for arsenic?"

"Yes, that is correct?"

"And do you treat patients?"

"No, I do not."

"If you do not treat patients, what then do you do?"

"I study chemistry and the effects of such on the body."

"Do you use humans for this or animals?"

"We use animals to determine some of the effects."

"And would you say that the anatomy of an animal is the same as and reacts the same as that of a human being when it receives a dose of medication?"

"The primates - yes."

"And when you received the organs, what were your exact instructions?"

"I was commissioned to review the organs sent to me for evidence of arsenic poisoning."

Mr. Bridgeman looked as if a light bulb went off in his head. "Ah, I see. And so you proceeded to look for arsenic and nothing else that would have caused the death of Mr. Vanderhoof. Meaning, if you were only employed to look for one specific item, how can you be certain that it was the arsenic that killed him?"

"There was a quantity of arsenic present that would have killed a person."

"But how do you know that for certain, Sir? You stated that you only test on animals and that you looked for no other poison. In fact, you stated you were told specifically to look for arsenic. Can you state, without a doubt, that there was nothing else in the body that could have caused his death?"

"I am certain it was poisoning by arsenic."

"And what of the condition of the organs, Doctor?"

"That was done by the Coroner."

"Doctor, would you have this court believe that you turned a blind eye to the conditions of the organs and simply searched them for arsenic and nothing else?"

"That was my commission, yes."

"How could you even be certain they were the organs of William Vanderhoof? Were you present when they were extracted from the body?"

"I was not."

"So, you did not examine the condition of the organs, or search the organs for any other substance, or even determine that these were the organs of Mr. William Vanderhoof. But, you state under oath that it was arsenic poisoning?"

"According to the medical literature, as the Doctor before me mentioned,...."

"What medical literature?"

"The Medical Journal. It discussed arsenic and the effects on the human body, the symptoms of arsenic poisoning, and the quantity necessary to poison a person." He held up the book that he had taken with him to the stand.

"And you are suggesting that this book was your authority on your conclusion?"

"This book added to my conclusions, yes."

"May I suggest to you, Sir, that we do not know the credentials of this author, and to enter this into evidence is equivalent to someone stating that they are an attorney and putting their opinions into print. And furthermore, to enter this into evidence under that presumption would be irresponsible based on that fact alone."

"Objection!" James Kellogg shouted.

"On what grounds?" the Judge asked.

"That book is regarded highly in the medical community, and its author is well known."

"Sustained."

Mr. Bridgeman turned to the Judge. "Your Honor, we cannot cross-examine the author of this book. To admit this book into evidence would be reckless."

"Do not tell me how to run my court, Mr. Bridgeman! Proceed with the witness."

"I am done with the witness."

The prosecution stood. "The Prosecution now calls Mr. Thomas Vanderhoof."

Thomas stood up. He looked tired, and the steps that he took showed the weight that the death of his son and this trial was having on him. With a heavy sigh, he sat down and glanced over at Lizzy. She stared straight ahead, not showing any sign of weakness.

"Mr. Vanderhoof, I would like to ask you about the night that your son, William, died. Can you please tell the court about an incident that occurred when the doctor pronounced that your son had passed on. I am referring to the incident between the accused and Mr. John Chapman."

Thomas drew in a deep breath. "Well, we had all been standing there for some time. William was complaining that he couldn't breathe, and he was flailing about with the covers. Sometimes he put them on, and sometimes he put them off. He continually called for Lizzy over and over even when she was there. He said nothing else but Lizzy, Lizzy. For the most part, she was in the room, but as the night grew on, she became impatient waiting on the Doctor and Mr. Chapman, and she spent some time staring out the window. Finally, she saw them and went down to the main floor to greet them. The Doctor came up, but Lizzy did not. Neither did Mr. Chapman. I sent my daughter, Sarah, to fetch her because I felt that the time of

Willie's death was drawing nigh. After Lizzy came into the room, followed by Mr. Chapman, the doctor informed us of Willie's passing. At that moment, Lizzy said, Oh John, do not leave me and fainted. He, Mr. Chapman, caught her because he was standing behind her. He carried her to the nearby bed. Then he proceeded to place cool clothes upon her chest as the women were tending to her."

"Mr. Chapman was touching Mrs. Elizabeth Vanderhoof's bosom?"

"Yes. It was a familiarity that one takes with a wife and not an employer."

"Why do you think this testimony to be of importance to this court, Mr. Vanderhoof?"

"I believe it shows the reason for Elizabeth to want William out of the way."

"Objection!"

"What grounds?"

"Pure speculation, Your Honor."

"Sustained."

The Prosecutor turned back toward the witness. "Thank you, Mr. Vanderhoof. I may call you later for other questions. Mr. Bridgeman, you may proceed."

Attorney Bridgeman stood, placing his hands on the table in front of him. "Mr. Vanderhoof, do you believe that Mrs. Vanderhoof was under a great deal of duress the moment her husband was pronounced dead?"

"Yes, I am sure she was. I would like to believe that she was."

"Do you think that people under duress could say things that wouldn't normally be said?"

160

"I guess that could be true, yes."

"Is it possible that since she had just come from having a conversation with Mr. Chapman to then hearing her husband pronounced dead that she could have simply mixed her words?"

"If that were all, yes. But what of the cloth that he placed upon her chest?"

"Yes, what of that? An act committed in front of all the others in the room. There was nothing hidden. Did Mr. Chapman give you the reason for his actions."

"He said he learned the medical skills in the army."

"I see. And you didn't believe that to be the truth?"

"I didn't know what to believe. It was improper to take such liberties."

"Thank you, Mr. Vanderhoof. I am done questioning this witness."

Mr. Kellogg stood up again, "I would like to call Sarah Vanderhoof."

Sarah stood smugly and walked briskly to the witness chair. After saying her oath, she looked scornfully over at Elizabeth.

"Mrs. Sarah Vanderhoof, would you please tell this court what you heard the night of the passing of your brother?"

"You just heard my father testify that Elizabeth went down to meet the doctor and Mr. Chapman, whom I might add is not in this courtroom today. When my father sent me to fetch Lizzy, I overheard her telling Mr. Chapman that it didn't take this long with Nathan, to which he replied for her remember the goal. They were talking very quietly and closely, too closely. As my father said, there was a familiarity between the two of them. Why even the night before William died we were all at the farm doing the chores, taking turns sitting with Willie, and trying to help where we could. I was upstairs sitting with Willie when Mr. Chapman came in. He was tired from the chores and lay down sideways on the second bed in the room. Shortly after he did, Elizabeth came in, and she did the same thing, but next to Mr. Chapman! She did it right there in the room by her dying husband!"

"Thank you, Sarah. Your witness, Mr. Bridgeman."

"Miss Vanderhoof," the Defense began, "do you like Elizabeth Vanderhoof?"

"No, I do not."

"And why is that?"

"She is a vile person, and she killed my brother, just like she killed her first husband, Nathan Salisbury."

"Miss Vanderhoof, are you aware of the cause of the death of Mr. Salisbury?"

"I am. He died in the same manner as my brother."

"Are you certain of this?"

"That is what I have heard."

"And have you seen the death certificate of Mr. Nathan Salisbury?"

"No, I did not, but I ..."

"Did you also hear that to testify under oath means to tell the truth at all times? Hearing something, Miss Vanderhoof, as in the speculation of the cause of Mr. Salisbury's death and then repeating that speculation as fact, isn't necessarily telling the truth at all times, is it?"

She didn't reply but just stared at him as if she wanted to speak but dared not.

"Miss Vanderhoof, how do you think you can tell this courtroom truthful statements about the accused if you are prejudiced against her?"

"I am not prejudiced."

"Aren't you? You just said that she is a vile person, and she killed your brother and her first husband. Those are statements with the first being subjective and neither proven by this court. Therefore, since you have twice now in the matter of a few minutes given untruthful statements, how can this court believe that you heard a conversation between Mrs. Vanderhoof and Mr. Chapman the night of Mr. Vanderhoof's death?"

"Because it happened!"

"I see. Just like Nathan Salisbury's death that you mentioned earlier; the speculation to which you have no fact but simply heard." He did not wait for her to respond but walked away and said, "No further questions, Your Honor."

"If there are no objections, we will reconvene tomorrow," the Judge stated. The court began to murmur as Elizabeth was led away by the Sherriff.

Chapter 15
Conversation by Fireside

It was late in the evening, as John Chapman sat near the fire in the home of his father, Samuel, attempting to warm himself from the chill of the day. He had just come back from Elizabeth's farm where he had been tending the animals in her absence.

"John, how long are you going to continue to hang around the Vanderhoof farm? Don't you realize that you are bringing more attention to yourself?"

"Father, there's nobody to care for the livestock, and I cannot let them starve. Lizzy's mother said she sent word to her family in Ohio for help. She's hoping some will come soon."

"John, I went to the trial again today. It's not looking positive for Elizabeth. I fear that you will be caught up in this somehow through your acquaintance with her."

"There is nothing to fear, Sir. They already let me go. There was nothing to hold me on or tie me to William's death."

"Yes, I know they let you go. What if they find a reason to come back after you. You are a young man, John. You have a life to live. I think you should consider this."

"Consider what, Father?"

"Consider leaving the area, John. You can leave here, and I can sell the farm and follow you at that time. Your mother would have wanted to see you go and start a family somewhere."

"Father! What of Lizzy?"

"What do you mean, 'what of Lizzy'? She is no good, John."

"I will not have you say such a thing!"

"John, you aren't using your reasoning. I implore you to leave and forget about her. You will thank me someday for this advice."

"I cannot leave."

"But why, son? Why can you not go and never look back towards that wretched woman?"

"Because that wretched woman is my wife!"

Samuel gasped and lurched forward in his chair. "Dear Almighty God, please tell me it is not the truth that you speak! Please, John, tell me it is not the truth!"

"It is the truth, Father, and I will not have another word about leaving."

"John," Samuel's tone suddenly became very serene, almost eerily serene. "There is something that I have been holding back from telling you. I had not wanted to bring this information to you so that I could spare you the pain of hearing it. But I fear this situation now warrants it. I beg you to hear me out, my son."

John crinkled his brow, "What is it?"

"Johnny, I am an old man, but I have learned a great many things in my age. And with my wisdom came the understanding of when to act upon things that I have learned and when to stay silent. This is a time to act upon it. Johnny, I knew old Mr. Salisbury, Nathan's father. When you and Nathan were in the military, Mr. Salisbury and I used to spend a great many days after Sunday meeting talking to take up the time of loneliness and worry for our sons. There was a time when we discussed

166

Elizabeth, Nathan's wife at the time. Mr. Salisbury seemed surprised that I stated I didn't quite know young Elizabeth, and he thought I ought to know her because you seemed to be well acquainted with her. I asked him how that could be, and he indicated that you came around now and then. So I thought to myself, how could my son be around now and then? It seemed odd to me at the time, and I stored that in memory. Then there was the time when he mentioned that he had overheard a conversation between you and Elizabeth. It seemed you had been discussing the law concerning property rights of a widow."

Samuel stood up and walked closer to the fireplace. He stared for a moment into the fire and then turned back towards John, who had remained quiet. "Old Mr. Salisbury died shortly after that, and oddly enough, Nathan's health began to fail as well. I don't believe Elizabeth counted on William entering the picture, did she? He seemed to be around all the time. In places where he, too, may have overheard conversations. It was a quick wedding for them, wasn't it? Shall I continue?"

"Stop! What you are saying is foolishness!"

"Is it? Do you think me an old fool, John? Now, I could go on with my story, or I can repeat what I told you earlier. You need to leave. The Vanderhoof's are a powerful family, Johnny. Elizabeth will not survive this trial. You can be assured of that."

"But she is my wife. I love her. I have always loved her."

"Where were you married?"

"Old Mr. Phillips on the prairie married us before he died"

"John, my son, they will tie you to the murder thru marriage to Lizzy! Have you no sense? Have I ever advised you to do anything that was not to your benefit?"

"No."

"John, the prosecution will call you to testify, and when you testify, you need to keep in mind your future. And then after your testimony, go. Go as far away from this place as you can. Forget Elizabeth Vanderhoof. Forget your time with her. Start a life somewhere else. You will find someone to share that life with. You will find a good woman, John."

John sat back in the chair and stared into the fire. When suddenly there was a rapping at the door.

Samuel walked over and opened the door. Standing on the front porch was a man unknown to both Samuel and John. He was a young man about John's age. He was dark-haired with dark eyes to match. His jawline was sharp and unshaven.

"Mr. Chapman?"

"Yes, I am Samuel Chapman."

"My name is Luke Unruh, Sir. Would John be at home this evening? I need to speak to him."

"Yes, Mr. Unruh, he is here. Come in, out of the cold."

Luke walked in, removed his hat, and shook the snow off of his black woolen coat. He spied John standing near the fireplace and walked straight over to him, stretching out his hand. "John Chapman, I am Luke Unruh. I need to speak with you, Sir."

"Have we made acquaintance before?" John asked.

"No, Sir, we haven't. May I sit down?"

"Please, do."

"Mr. Chapman, may I call you John?"

"Yes."

"John, I am here to talk to you about Elizabeth Vanderhoof."

"And what of her, Mr. Unruh?"

"Well, I record deeds and documents for the court. And obviously, the news of what has occurred with Mrs. Vanderhoof and yourself reached the papers, and I have read of it. And as I read, I began to recall the day Mr. and Mrs. Vanderhoof came to the court office to switch the title on the property that they owned. I thought to myself, 'Is this the couple that was in here this past summer?' And as curiosity got the better of me, I decided to take a trip to the courthouse to hear some of the testimony for myself."

"What is your point, Mr. Unruh?" John said getting noticeably irritated with the interruption to his evening.

"The point is that when the Sheriff brought in Mrs. Vanderhoof, that was not the woman who came into the clerk's office with Mr. William Vanderhoof."

Samuel perked up. He had been casually listening and filling his pipe with tobacco and stopped in mid-action. "My good man, please repeat what you have just uttered."

"The woman that came into my office to record the change to the deed on the property was not the same woman that was brought into the courtroom to stand trial for the murder."

John stepped forward. His eyes widened a bit. "Are you sure it was William Vanderhoof that came in?"

"Yes, I am sure. I had run into Mr. Thomas Vanderhoof not too far back in the General Store, and he was with his son William. We were introduced. But William was not with that woman who is on trial for his murder."

"Can you describe the woman he was with?" Samuel questioned.,

"I can not only describe her; I can point her out. She was in the courtroom. I saw her there, but I do not believe she saw me."

John began to pace. "You saw this woman in the courtroom?"

"Yes, she was sitting next to Mr. Thomas Vanderhoof."

"Did she have dark hair or lighter reddish hair?"

"Dark hair. They left together in a buggy. I heard him call her dear when he helped her up into the buggy. She seemed several years younger than him, so I believed her to be his daughter."

"Tryphena! It was Tryphena!"

"Mr. Unruh, what was it they were there for?"

"They were transferring the property deed on Mrs. Vanderhoof's acreage. It was fifty acres; I believe. The property name was deeded to a Nathan and Elizabeth Salisbury, and the woman that I believed to be Elizabeth Vanderhoof, deeded it to Mr. William Vanderhoof."

"I don't understand," Samuel interjected. "Wasn't the property already his through marriage?"

"Not in the State of Michigan, Sir. The property belonged to Mr. Salisbury and upon passing it became his widow's property. The laws have changed, and they allow a woman now to own property apart from her husband. It does not revert to his family. So the acreage belonged completely to Mrs. Elizabeth Vanderhoof, and Mr. Vanderhoof only had use of it while they were married."

Samuel's voice got a bit quieter. "So if the property was recorded in William's name, then he could do with it as he pleased without her approval. The only way for her to regain this property would be if he were to die."

"Father! Do not say such a thing!"

"Tell me, Mr. Unruh," Samuel continued. "Would there have been any way for Mrs. Vanderhoof to have found this out?"

"Yes, Sir. After the deed is recorded, we would have sent a post of the transaction. So if Mrs. Vanderhoof intercepted that post, she would have found the information out."

John sat back down as if the weight of the world had just been dumped on his shoulders. He let his head fall back onto the back of the chair. After a few moments, John looked at Luke Unruh and squinted his eyes. "Why have you come here, Mr. Unruh? What benefit to yourself does this have?"

"Mr. Chapman, I record other things besides land certificates. I also record marriage certificates." He stopped and kept his eyes fixed upon John momentarily. "It seems to me that your wife is in a bit of a spot while I seem to be in the position of good fortune."

"You scoundrel!"

"Scoundrel or not, Mr. Chapman. I can either help your wife or not. The choice is yours."

"Just what are you proposing?"

"Well, Sir, if I testify that I have recorded the deed for Mr. Vanderhoof and sent the post, then it leads to the suspicion that Mrs. Vanderhoof intercepted the post and has a motive for murder; a murder to which you are tied to by association. And that association should have been only as of the hired hand. If the association becomes one of a secret lover and now a husband, it could, how should I say it, cause complications?"

John jumped up and grabbed Luke by the jacket. "How dare you come in here and..."

"John, stop!" Samuel yelled. "This man talks sense. You may not like it, but that is what it is! He is offering you an opportunity, and you cannot see it! Unhand him and hear him out!"

Luke straightened his jacket and brushed back his hair. "Mr. Chapman, I believe my silence can be purchased and have your marriage to Mrs. Vanderhoof disappear for forty acres of your northern property plus a breeding stallion."

"That is outrageous! And how am I assured that if I agree to your terms that you would carry out your part?"

"I will bring you the book with the record of the marriage, and you could destroy that page here. You would then not be tied to Mrs. Vanderhoof in the event the prosecution would look in this direction."

"We will accept your terms, Mr. Unruh," Samuel said.

"Father! Do not speak for me! Think of what you are saying!"

Samuel walked up to John and put his hand on his shoulder with a firm grasp. "Clear the fog from your head, my son! This is a God-send, even if it seems evil now. The best thing you can do is to take this man's offer and do as we talked about earlier! Johnny, if you ever trusted me, trust me now!"

John's countenance changed from anger to defeat. He nodded his head and sat back down on the chair. He stared into the fire momentarily and then with a crackle in his voice said, "I accept your terms, Mr. Unruh."

Chapter 16
The Conclusion

The next day proved to be as well attended as the prior. The townspeople had been arriving since early that morning despite the light snow falling. It seemed that everyone wanted to get a seat and not have to stand in the back.

Thomas and Tryphena arrived early as well, and there had been seats saved for them in the front of the room. As he and his wife walked towards their seats, many of the other men stopped him to offer condolences on the death of his son and to say how sorry they were about the accusation. The woman would chime in with the same words, 'we just never suspected Lizzy.'

Elizabeth arrived with the Sheriff and walked towards her seat at the table with her attorney. Just as the day before when she entered the room, all the idle chatter stopped, and all eyes turned on her. Her hair was, once again, pulled back in a tight bun revealing her pale white skin and blue eyes. The dress that she wore was the same as the day before only a bit wrinkled. She looked tired today and did not walk with the vigor that she did the day prior. Her walk was slower and lighter, and she did not gaze upon the crowd. Instead, she just sat and fixed her eyes on the ground in front of her.

Mr. Kellogg, the prosecutor, walked in, accompanied by the Judge. Both were seated, as the Judge pounded the gavel, once again, calling the court into order. The outside doors were closed, and no others were allowed to enter.

"Is the prosecution ready this morning?" The Judge asked.

"Yes, Your Honor. The prosecution calls its' first witness, Mr. John Chapman."

There was a loud noise as if the entire room took in a deep breath at the same time. The Sheriff walked down the center aisle towards the doors, opened them, and stepped outside. He returned in short order with John Chapman, who had been waiting outside in his buggy. As the Sheriff and John walked back inside, all the men stepped aside. John walked up towards the witness seat. Lizzy looked up for the first time since she had come into the room that morning. He met her gaze briefly and then looked away, nervously.

"Mr. Chapman," the prosecution began, "please tell the court how you know Mrs. Vanderhoof."

He swallowed hard. "I came to work for her husband after he took sick."

"And how did you know he needed help?"

"It was mentioned around town."

"And you were not a friend to Mrs. Vanderhoof prior? Had never known her prior?"

"No."

"No? There are witnesses who claim that there was a familiarity between both of you."

John said nothing. He just looked at the attorney.

"Have you nothing to say to that, Mr. Chapman?"

"I didn't hear a question, Sir. I heard a statement."

Mr. Chapman, have you ever possessed a photo of Mrs. Vanderhoof?"

John suddenly remembered his watch and became very nervous.

"Mr. Chapman, did you hear the question?"

"Yes, I have a photo of Elizabeth."

"And why, Sir, would you have a photograph of a married woman if there was no prior connection between the two of you and you were not familiar with one another?"

"I found it.

"You found it? Just lying around like the dust? Where did you find such a photo?"

"When I was in the war, I served with Mr. Salisbury. When he was injured, they sent him home. He left a bag behind and in it was a photo."

"A photo of a married woman that her husband was carrying around? This is something you took?"

"Yes, but I had planned to send it back to him."

"But you never did. Is that correct, Mr. Chapman?"

"Yes, that is correct."

"Why did you not return the photo?"

"Mr. Salisbury passed away."

"And what became of this photo?

"I had It with me for many years, and then I lost the bag that it was in."

"I see. Mr. Chapman, a conversation was overheard between you and Mrs. Vanderhoof in which she was said to make the statement 'it didn't take this long with Nathan.' Do you recall that statement?

"Yes."

"And what did she mean by that?"

"Objection! Speculation." Mr. Bridgeman shouted.

"Sustained." The Judge nodded.

"Mr. Chapman, what was your understanding of that statement?"

"I understood it to mean that Nathan, her first husband, had not suffered so long before his death. It seemed William was really suffering."

"Did it strike you odd that she would say that to you?"

"No."

"Mr. Chapman, you worked for the Vanderhoof's for a while. Did they have rats in the home?"

John paused and looked down. Then he looked over at Lizzy whose gaze was fixated on his.

"Mr. Chapman, do you need me to repeat the question?"

"No."

"I'm confused, Mr. Chapman, did you mean no, you do not need me to repeat the question or no, there were not rats about the house."

"No, to both. I do not need you to repeat the question, and I did not see rats about the house. But I also was not in the home very often."

"But you were in the home. Was it ever mentioned to you that there were rats?"

"No." He looked over at Lizzy who was now looking back down at the ground.

"Mr. Chapman, there was a statement overheard the night of Mr. Vanderhoof's death that was directed at you. It is stated that Elizabeth Vanderhoof said, 'oh John, do not leave me.' Do you recall this, and what was your interpretation of this statement?"

"I do not recall this."

176

"You do not recall this? Other witnesses have testified and are willing to testify that they heard this, also. But, you, the person it was directed to, does not recall this?"

"I do not."

"When she fainted, you were quick to come to her aid. Why?"

"Any decent person would."

"And would any decent person place a cloth on the bosom of a woman that was another man's wife and take that familiarity with her?"

"I was attempting to help as the ladies wanted a cool cloth on her chest."

"I see. And yet there was no prior connection between the two of you? That is very interesting, Mr. Chapman. It is interesting because you state there was no familiarity between you, yet she confided to you about the suffering of her husband, called out to you before fainting, slept next to you at the barn at Redding Mill, and is rumored to have married you. So, I ask you again, Mr. Chapman, did you know Mrs. Elizabeth Vanderhoof on other terms, as a man would know a woman?"

John swallowed hard and did not look up either at the prosecutor or at Lizzy. He heard her voice in his head saying, 'promise me you will not tell anyone we were married.' Then he said, "No, I did not know Mrs. Vanderhoof on familiar terms."

"No more questions."

Silently, Elizabeth breathed a sigh of relief.

Now it was the defense who stood. Mr. Bridgeman tugged on his brown vest. "Mr. Chapman, you say you did not see rats about the house. At what times were you in the home?"

"Usually for the meals. Mrs. Vanderhoof made the meals, and I took up quarters in the barn."

"So you were only there to eat? You did not go from room to room in the home?"

"No. The longest I stayed in the home was the night Mr. Vanderhoof died."

"And you were not looking for rats, were you?"

"No."

"So you cannot say with certainty that there were or were not rats in the home?"

"No."

"Did Mrs. Vanderhoof always tell you her business? I mean, if she would have been troubled by rats in the home, would this have been something she would have discussed with you?"

"No."

"So, therefore, it would be reasonable to state that there most certainly could have been rats in the house, and Mrs. Vanderhoof did not speak of them to you."

"Yes, that could be true."

"What was your ranking in the military?"

"I was a medical officer."

"So, helping Mrs. Vanderhoof after she fainted was a reaction, not a familiarity?"

"Yes."

"Thank you. You may be excused."

"One moment, please. The prosecution would like to question Mr. Chapman further, Your Honor."

"Very well," Judge Gilbert stated. "Proceed."

"Mr. Chapman, you just stated that you were a medical officer in the military. Did you have training before entering the military?"

"I did. I was preparing to become a physician."

"Oh, and why did you not continue after the service?"

"I didn't care for the profession."

"And in your training, did you receive training on medications?"

"What do you mean?"

"Did you receive training in what medicinal concoctions would help with different diseases?"

"Some."

"Did you ever study arsenic?"

John began to fidget with his hat that was in his lap. "I know where you are trying to lead, and the answer is no."

"No, to what, Mr. Chapman?"

"No, Elizabeth never asked me about arsenic for rats or anything else."

"I see. And what would draw you to that conclusion as to my line of questioning?"

"She is on trial for arsenic poisoning, isn't she? It is only logical that you would think she would have asked me about it based upon your line of questioning."

"My question was, are you familiar with the use of arsenic in common medical preparations? Only you concluded that I was inferring a connection between your knowledge and Elizabeth Vanderhoof's inquiry into it. And so I will ask you again. Are you familiar with the symptoms of poisoning using arsenic?"

"Objection!"

"On what grounds?"

"This witness is not a medical expert; therefore, his knowledge of arsenic is irrelevant."

"Sustained. You are dismissed, Mr. Chapman."

John stepped down quickly and began to make his way towards the center aisle that would lead to the outdoors and his waiting team of horse and wagon. But as he reached Elizabeth, he stopped momentarily. She looked at him, and he looked back at her, studying her beautiful face once more. Then he felt the tears begin to swell in his eyes, and he put his head down and walked out the door.

He was headed back home to gather his things that had been packed since the night before when he made a deal with Luke Unruh. As he cued the team to begin the journey, he glanced back at the courthouse once more. For a moment, he thought of Elizabeth and of recanting on his deal with Mr. Unruh, but his father's words filled his head. He turned away his glance from the courthouse and slapped the reins on the back of the horses for them to move. And as the horses pulled the buggy away from the building and away from Elizabeth, tears began to fall from his eyes. It would be the last time any of them would see or hear from John Chapman again.

Inside the courtroom, the prosecutor was up again, pacing back and forth. He placed his hands upon his hips, pulling back his suit coat from his sides. His golden watch chain dangled for onlookers to see. Then as if in a theatrical performance, he turned towards the room and said, "The State of Michigan calls to the witness stand, Elizabeth Vanderhoof."

Elizabeth didn't move. She sat frozen, almost shocked that she had been called. Her attorney shook her arm and leaned over towards her and whispered, "Go ahead, it will be okay."

Nervously, she stood and attempted to straighten her dress. There could have been a pin dropped and heard as the courtroom became deadly silent. Every eye was upon her as she moved forward, and the clicking of her boots upon the wooden floor even seemed to echo. The attorney stood waiting with the Bible in one hand, and as she approached, he put it in front of her. She placed her hand upon it.

The Judge cleared his throat and began, "Elizabeth Vanderhoof, do you swear to tell the truth, the whole truth, and nothing but the truth, so help you God?"

"I do," she said and slowly sat down. Now that she was at the front of the room looking out, she was overwhelmed by the size of the crowd and all the eyes staring at her. It was almost as if she could read their judgmental thoughts. She looked over at Thomas and Tryphena then at Sarah. They stared at her with no expression upon their face. These three people who had entertained her in their homes and helped in her home now sat staring at her with hate in their eyes. And the townspeople that she had attended Sunday meeting with chatted with, and known for years also sat staring at her as if they didn't recognize her. She looked away from them and toward the attorney as he began speaking.

"Mrs. Vanderhoof, we are here today because there is suspicion of wrongdoing on your part toward your husband, William Vanderhoof. It is the assertion of this court that you purchased arsenic and poisoned your husband pretending to give him his medicine. Do you deny this?"

"Yes, I deny this accusation."

"You deny purchasing the arsenic?"

"No, I do not deny it. I did purchase arsenic. I was told to purchase the arsenic by Dr. Mann. We had rats about the house, and he told me to get Rough on Rats, but that could not be found at the druggist. Then I asked for strychnine, and the druggist gave me arsenic."

"You asked for strychnine? Why strychnine? Why would you know that to be an effective cure for rats?"

"Dr. Mann told me if I could not locate Rough on Rats, to go after strychnine. I remember it clearly. The druggist forgot to mark it and took it back from my hand and said, 'Don't commit suicide.' I joked that if I did, he would hear about it."

"And what became of the arsenic powder?"

"I brought it home and mixed it as I was told and stored the rest away."

"And where did you store it?"

"In the cupboard."

"And what of the first time you purchased arsenic? I am of course referring to the time when you were married to Nathan Salisbury."

"I purchased it for Mr. Vanderhoof. He asked for it when he worked for us."

"You purchased it for William Vanderhoof? Your hired man at the time? And why did you purchase it for him?"

"William worked for Mr. Salisbury and me after the war, and he was staying in our barn. He stated there were rats in the barn and asked that I purchase it."

"Come, now, Mrs. Vanderhoof. Are you implying that Mr. Vanderhoof was not capable of purchasing this on his own?"

"I am not stating any such thing. Mr. Vanderhoof and I went to town for supplies. He was going to the feed store, and I went to the druggist. I purchased tooth powder for myself and arsenic for Mr. Vanderhoof."

"If that is the truth, Mrs. Vanderhoof, don't you believe that the receipt from the druggist would have stated that? The receipt only states that you purchased arsenic. How can you explain that?"

"I cannot. I don't understand why it would not have stated that I purchased tooth powder in addition to the arsenic, but I most certainly did."

"Can you prove that, Ma'am?"

"Can you not?" she said quickly.

"You are inferring that the druggist made a mistake; a man who is trained to be precise with the measurements of chemicals for medicinal purposes left out the notation of the purchase of tooth powder? So either the druggist is incompetent, or you are not truthful. Which is it?"

"The druggist must have forgotten to list the tooth powder," she stated emphatically.

"I see. Mrs. Vanderhoof, please tell the court how you came to know Mr. Vanderhoof."

"William Vanderhoof was my husband."

"That was not what I asked of you. I asked you how you came to know him before he was your husband?"

"I have known him for a long time. He worked for Nathan and me when Nathan became ill."

"Nathan Salisbury, your first husband, died in eighteen hundred seventy-six, didn't he?"

"Yes."

"To be exact, Mrs. Vanderhoof, he died in March of eighteen hundred seventy-six, and you married Mr. Vanderhoof in April of eighteen hundred seventy-six. Isn't that true, Mrs. Vanderhoof?"

"Yes."

"And isn't it also true that Mr. Salisbury died of a stomach ailment?"

"No, Mr. Salisbury was shot in the war and died of that injury sometime later."

"Isn't it true that there was some talk at that time that Mr. Salisbury died under unusual circumstances?"

"I know of no such thing."

"Isn't it true your child, Clara Bell, that you had with Mr. Salisbury also died of unusual circumstances?"

"No."

"And how did the child die?"

"Clara died of smallpox?"

"Isn't it true there was chatter surrounding her death as well?"

"I know of no such thing."

"Mr. Salisbury's father lived with you as well, correct?"

"Yes."

"He died shortly before his son, Nathan, did he not?

"Yes."

"He, too, died rather suddenly did he not?"

"He was elderly, Mr. Kellogg. And Sir, I am not slow of mind. I understand the unfavorable picture you are attempting to paint. However, my husband, Nathan, was shot in the war and had complications from that until he died. Our daughter was ill and contracted smallpox, which also took her life. William was sick for two years before he died. Two doctors singularly stated it was his heart that was failing. You would do well to paint the entire portrait, Sir!"

"I am well aware of the portrait I am painting Mrs. Vanderhoof! Tell me, how do you know Mr. John Chapman, the man who testified earlier that he did not see rats about the house. The man who was arrested with you?"

"He worked on the farm for Mr. Vanderhoof and me."

"Is it true that you knew Mr. Chapman when you were married to Mr. Salisbury?"

"No."

"No? You only met him recently?"

"Yes, after William became ill."

"Then I would like to show you something, Mrs. Vanderhoof." James Kellogg retrieved a watch from the desk where he had been sitting. He placed it in his palm and with an outstretched arm, asked, "Would you please open the watch and tell the court what you see?"

"It is a photo inside a watch."

"And would you tell this court who the picture is and owned the watch?"

"It is a picture of me, and I do not know who owned the watch. You handed it to me. It is the first time I have seen it."

"Then let me tell the court. This is a watch that was found in Mr. John Chapman's bag after the two of you were arrested." The courtroom erupted into talk.

"Order!" Judge Gilbert slammed the gavel down.

"Please tell the court why Mr. Chapman would have a photo of you inside his watch?" James Kellogg continued questioning.

"I do not know. It is his watch."

"Was it a gift from you?"

185

"No."

"Surely you were aware that he possessed your photo, did you not? And this very phot does show a bit of familiarity between the two of you, doesn't it?"

"No, and tell me why did you not ask Mr. Chapman if this watch belonged to him? Why did you not show him this photo? Why show it to me? I do not own it."

"Mrs. Vanderhoof, you have testified that there was no connection between you and Mr. Chapman, and I believe that to be a lie. This watch is a testimony of that fact."

"That watch could belong to you, for all I know. You could have acquired a photo of me and placed it in there to add to your theatrics here today."

"Mrs. Vanderhoof, is it not true that you did not want to be tied to an invalid such as Mr. Salisbury whose wound from the war left him unable to walk and unable to perform any husbandly duties? Mr. Vanderhoof offered you a way out of this situation. Isn't that true?"

"No."

"Isn't it true that William Vanderhoof wanted to sell your property to his father, Thomas, and the two of you had a falling out over this?"

"That is true. William wanted to sell the property, and I told him no."

"Why did you tell him no?"

"It was my property from my first husband. I was not going to give it to Thomas and Tryphena!"

"And why is that?"

Elizabeth looked down. The prosecutor repeated his statement.

"Why is that, Mrs. Vanderhoof, I ask you again."

"She had attempted an affair with my husband!"

"Liar!" Tryphena stood up and shouted. "You liar!"

"I do not lie! I heard the conversation between the two of you inside the barn. You wanted to be with William, and he told you no. He told you if you didn't stop that he would go to his father, your husband. You were angry with him. And it was you who mixed the powder that night that killed him. You went to my cupboard. You saw the rat poison. You gave him two doses the night he died so he wouldn't tell your dirty secret!"

"You liar!" she shouted again.

"Order! Order in this courtroom!" Mrs. Vanderhoof, please speak only to the attorney, and Mrs. Tryphena Vanderhoof, please do not speak in this courtroom unless you are asked.

Mr. Kellogg continued his assault. "Mrs. Vanderhoof, isn't it true that you were angry with William because he was pushing you to sell the property and then you became acquainted with Mr. Chapman and wanted William out of the way?"

"No."

"Mrs. Vanderhoof, how then do you account for the arsenic found in your husband's body?"

"I just told you. I believe Tryphena poisoned him. She had access to the poison that evening. She mixed his medicine, not I. And besides, I believe this entire trial to be based upon a lie."

"A lie?"

"I believe that the witnesses that were brought forth were paid. All because Thomas Vanderhoof wants my property. He came to me in my cell and asked me for the stallion and told me that I would need money to pay for this trial. He offered to purchase my property and the horse so that I would have money to defend myself. He never asked me how he could help or gave any indication that he believed my innocence. He was focused only upon his greed. And so, I believe not the witnesses. And I was not the last person to administer anything to my husband. Furthermore, there is not one person in this courtroom that can testify that they saw me harm Willie – not one, yet I sit here accused!"

"You sit here because the evidence supports the accusation! No more questions for now."

"Does the defense have any questions for Mrs. Vanderhoof?" The Judge asked.

"Not at this time."

Elizabeth looked over at Mr. Bridgeman, surprised by his response, and she rose to step down and walked over towards Mr. Bridgeman and whispered into his ear.

"Your honor," he addressed the Judge, "Mrs. Vanderhoof needs to take a break."

"Very well, we will break for fifteen minutes."

Elizabeth was escorted toward the outhouse. She reached into her dress and pulled out a piece of paper; the paper that she had retrieved from her bag the night of her arrest. It read, 'Berrien County Recorder of Deeds: Transfer of property from Elizabeth Salisbury Vanderhoof to William Vanderhoof, NE corner, section fourteen, fifty acres.' This was the very document that Luke Unruh had spoken to John Chapman about. A document that nobody knew she was in possession of and the very document that had been drafted behind her back and without her approval. Quickly, she tore the paper into tiny pieces and threw them down the outhouse port. She shoved her finger down her throat, and in the distance, the bystanders could hear her vomiting.

The trial lasted for three more days. Numerous witnesses were called upon, and then came the day that the jury was asked its opinion.

"And how does the jury find the defendant, Elizabeth Vanderhoof?"

"We find the defendant guilty according to the charge."

Elizabeth's knees weakened, and she grabbed the table in front of her. The Judge turned to her and said, "Elizabeth Vanderhoof you have been found guilty of the murder of your husband, William. You are fortunate in that the State of Michigan does not put to death any of those convicted; otherwise, you would be sentenced to hang from your neck until you were dead. Therefore, I sentence you to solitary confinement in the State Penitentiary for the rest of your life

Back in Vandalia, Robert walked into his home from a hard day's work. He found Lynn where he had left her earlier with her foot propped up from the surgery.

"So, what have you done all day? And better yet, have you stayed off that foot?" he asked.

"Oh, not much. Read my diaries, did some research on the computer, and worked on writing a book about something I found in the diary."

"Anything interesting?"

"Not really. Well, there was this trial, but you probably wouldn't be interested in it."

"Well, I'm glad you were a good girl and got some rest. We have an anniversary coming up, and I would like to take you dancing! But for now, I am going to walk the dog." He kissed her and headed out the back door with their dog, Napoleon. Lynn picked up her cell phone and dialed a number.

"Agent Weber speaking."

"Hey, it's Lynn. I don't have a lot of time to explain, but I want to have a renewal of my wedding vows. Can you set that up?"

"Renewal?" The voice at the other end said. "Don't you have to be married for real to have a renewal?"

"Yes, and oh, this time, let's use a real preacher."

T he End Maybe...Turn the Page

Addendum

As stated in the Preface, this is a fictional novel based upon certain factual details that did occur between 1883 and 1888. The following bullet points are facts, in no particular order, that were in this novel and upon which the author built around and based the rest of this work.

- Elizabeth Vanderhoof was arrested, stood trial, pled not guilty, but was convicted of the murder of her husband, William.
- She was sentenced to solitary confinement at the State Penitentiary for the rest of her life. She was later moved to the Detroit House of Corrections.
- After serving four years of her sentence, an appeal to the Michigan State Supreme Court cited error of the lower court and overturned the previous conviction of her sentence, thus releasing her back to Berrien County for re-trial, with bail set at $3,000. (A portion of the actual excerpt from the Supreme Court's decision is included at the end of this book.)
- Her bail of $3,000 was equivalent to over $74,000 in today's currency.
- William Vanderhoof was the hired hand for Nathan Salisbury, Elizabeth's first husband.
- Witnesses testified that William Vanderhoof did flail and suffer before his death.

- Drs. Palmer, Hendricks, and Prescott, Professors of Anatomy and Chemistry did testify in the trial of Elizabeth Vanderhoof.

- Professor Prescott stated that he found in the stomach, liver, and kidneys, "the minimum quantity of arsenic sufficient to cause death."

- Dr. Palmer stated that he could not determine the cause of death.

- Dr. Prescott sent a letter to the Prosecuting Attorney after the finding of arsenic in Mr. Vanderhoof's organs. This letter is what prompted the arrest of Elizabeth Vanderhoof.

- Dr. Henderson did state the William "had nervousness about him and looked around the room with a wild-like gaze and swung his legs."

- It was proven that Elizabeth did purchase a half-ounce of arsenic from the druggist, Captain Sterns, about the middle of September 1883.

- There is no truth that she purchased arsenic before the death of her first husband, Nathan.

- There were over eighty witnesses who testified at the trial.

- The courthouse was packed every day of the trial.

- Several witnesses testified that there was familiarity between Elizabeth and John Chapman.

- Several witnesses testified that Elizabeth called out John's name before fainting after hearing the pronouncement of William's death.

- Witnesses also testified that both Elizabeth and John lay upon the same bed together, although horizontal in positions.
- Clapp and Bridgeman were attorneys for Elizabeth Vanderhoof.
- Moses Taggart was the attorney for the State of Michigan.
- Elizabeth married Nathan Salisbury on November 5, 1865.
- Nathan died on March 3, 1876. His probate was on April 7, 1876.
- Elizabeth was granted $500 from his estate. This is equivalent to over $11,500 in today's currency.
- There was speculation surrounding Nathan Salisbury's death, but no formal charges were ever brought against Elizabeth.
- There is no evidence that Nathan ever suffered from a gunshot wound. There was only a small reference found stating that he was a cripple.
- The body of Nathan Salisbury was never disinterred.
- Elizabeth's child did die eight months after Nathan died.
- Elizabeth married William Vanderhoof on May 18, 1876, two months after the death of Nathan Salisbury. Her direct testimony to a reporter for the Chicago Tribune, March 4, 1884, shows she contradicted court documents stating, "*I married William Vanderhoof nine years ago, and about fourteen months after the death of my first husband.*

My first husband died in March, and our little girl in the following August."

- Elizabeth stated in the interview with the Chicago Tribune reporter that *"Mr. Vanderhoof was taken sick the 8th of May last. He thought he was stricken with paralysis. Old Mr. Phillips on the prairie died the same day of paralysis that my husband was taken sick. I gave him some medicine prescribed for myself. I had been troubled with liver complaint, and this was a tonic. From this time on, he complained of his heart fluttering. He complained of feelings of suffocation."*

- Dr. Mann was the physician who attended to William.

- Thomas Vanderhoof sent for Dr. Dodd of Buchanan who determined that William's trouble was heart disease and lung difficulty.

- Dr. Dodd changed the medication and gave it to Elizabeth in a bulk powder so that she had to mix it for her husband.

- The druggist who sold her the arsenic did state for her not to commit suicide with the arsenic powder.

- John Chapman was initially arrested and then released as there was no evidence to hold him.

- No records could be found to determine what had ever happened to John Chapman.

- There was speculation about an alleged marriage between Elizabeth and John, but it was never proven.

194

- Both the Vanderhoof's and the Salisbury's were early settlers to the area.

- Those present at the death of William were Thomas and Tryphena, Samuel Chapman, Elizabeth, and a few others.

- Tryphena was the step-mother to William and did administer the medication to him the night of his death.

- An article from the St. Louis Post dispatch dated Friday, July 13, 1888 stated, "*Mrs. William Vanderhoof of Galien, Michigan, who was sentenced to life imprisonment for poisoning her husband, has after four years of untiring effort proved that she is innocent and that the man's step-mother was guilty of the crime.*" The author found no evidence that Tryphena Vanderhoof was ever tried for the alleged crime.

- Thomas Vanderhoof was the executor of the estate of William Hardy, Elizabeth's father.

- Thomas did tell Elizabeth that he wanted to have a certain horse that William owned. So much so that she "*had to go to the Probate Judge and was told to keep the barn locked and hold on the horse.*" According to Elizabeth, she, John, and her mother were "*up all night watching to prevent them from getting the horse.*"

- There is no truth that Thomas Vanderhoof ever intended to have or own the land the Elizabeth owned.

- The charges of wrong-doing by Elizabeth, resulting in the death of William, were leveled by William's sister, and that is what initiated the investigation and ultimate disinterment of his body.

- William's sister's name was not Sarah. Sarah was the name of his biological mother.

- The names of her children from Nathan Salisbury were Clara Bell, Lydia Jane, and Jennie Lind. There are several references to a Jane Vanderhoof.

- Elizabeth's mother cared for her children while she was in prison.

- William was given quinine and calomel; both are highly toxic drugs. Calomel contains mercury and is known as the "beautiful black poison." It is not used in modern medicine today.

- William's symptoms included: burning in the stomach, coldness, pain around the heart, numbness of the lower extremities, dizzy spells, feelings of suffocation, lung pain, fever, and the inability to lie on his left side.

- The night of his death, it was reported that his pulse was increased, his tongue was slimy, he had a white marbled appearance on his skin, and he had diarrhea.

- William Vanderhoof had complained to his doctor about heart pain for up to three years prior.

- A neighbor, Frank Batton, testified that William's eyes were bloated, face swelled, and eyelids and face were yellow.

- During the trial, it was thought that Elizabeth was pregnant.
- Elizabeth eventually sold her property pay for her court bills.
- In 1926, Elizabeth Vanderhoof was formally pardoned by the Governor acknowledging that she served four years in prison from 1884-1888.
- She died January 29, 1927, one year after her official pardon.
- If hanging had been a state penalty, she would have been hanged for a crime that she was later pardoned for.

To the knowledge and research of this author, the case was never re-tried, as it was based solely on circumstantial evidence to begin with. *However, the search goes on*.

I bet you are wondering:

What happened to Maggie Martin? Was the crime ring ever brought down? What does Robert do with the papers? Where did Sarah go when she left her father's home so suddenly? When did Lizzy find out that John had left her? And several other question.......**There is a sequel planned. Watch for it**!

A Portion of The Supreme Court's Decision is listed below. You can read the rest of it at:

71 Mich 158, 173:39 NW 28 (1888)

...... *"from the middle of September to the time of his death, and also the existence, long before, of these spells, which indicated, As Vanderhoof and the physician, thought, heart trouble. No reference was made either to the condition of the heart as before noted or the enlargement of the right ventricle, as testified by Dr. Hendrix. It was the duty of the prosecution to lay the whole case of this man's sickness and death, as they had made it, before these experts, or so much of it as had an important bearing upon his death, instead of picking out detached portions of it to suit their theories of the case. The whole of the undisputed important facts of the last sickness, and developed at the post mortem, should have been embraced or summarized in the hypothetical questions leading to and inquiring as to the cause of death. But this was not done, nor fairly attempted to be done. Important facts were left out, and some things inserted that were not factors, and could not consistently be claimed to be facts within the testimony. It is impossible to particularize all these omissions or the insertions of facts. Nor is it necessary to do so. Nearly all the hypothetical questions propounded by the people to the medical experts confined the symptoms of the deceased to 12 or 20 hours before his death, ignoring his condition and ailments previous thereto; and gave only a partial statement of the results of the post mortem. The difficulty of the heart, with which Vanderhoof* thought he suffered so long, was studiously avoided, as was the diseased condition of the heart as shown by the autopsy. I believe that even in a civil case, all the undisputed facts of a case must be included in a hypothetical question, both as a matter of sound principle and of reason and justice. Neither party has a right to discard any important undisputed facts because the insertion of such fact may alter or vary the answer or opinion of the witness to the prejudice of such party. Expert testimony is only allowed upon the theory that it is necessary in some case, where the jury cannot be supposed to comprehend the significance of facts shown by other testimony which needs scientific or peculiar explanation by those who do comprehend it. People v. Millard, 523 Michigan, 75, 18 N.W. Rep. 562. This explanation cannot well be given so as to be of any worth or usefulness, especially in a diagnosis of disease, without all the facts known to exist are made the basis and foundation of the opinion. So much may a single fact or symptom.....this being the fact which cannot be gainsaid justice and humanity demand that in a criminal case, where life, liberty, and reputation are the issues, the prosecuting officer in examining an expert should lay before such expert fairly and fully every material fact undisputed that can have a possible bearing upon the opinion of such witness. To permit as was done in this case, a culling of facts to suit the purposes of conviction to be propounded in hypothesis to the experts, and then to instruct the jury that the only way to contradict the opinion of the experts is by the opinion of other experts, is to deny a fair trial; and in a case where the accused was unable to procure experts because of poverty, would be an outrage, and a reproach to our jurisprudence. It has time and time again been said by this court that the duty of the

199

prosecuting attorney is not to distort or withhold evidence in order to convict. He is the representative of the people of which the accused is one, and his duty is to fairly and fully lay before the jury every fact and circumstance known to him to exist, without regard to whether such fact tends to establish the guilt or innocence of the respondent. This is his whole duty, no more, no less. Complaint is also made that while the examination of the witness by the prosecution, and the entire conduct of the people's case, went upon the theory that the deceased came to his death from acute or subacute poisoning to whit the administration of large doses or fatal does from 12 to 24 hours before death, and this was the case the defense was called upon to meet and did combat, yet the circuitry Judge submitted the case to the jury upon the theory of slow or chronic poison, commencing first in September and that he misstated the testimony also in so doing. We do not think the charge is fairly open to this complaint. The court, in stating what the people claimed, it is true, did state a case of slow poisoning, and perhaps, in numeration, the facts claimed by the people mentioned some things that were not proven. But the claim of the people, as made in their opening or in their argument to the jury, is not before us, and the court may have correctly stated the claim as made by them. It is evident from an examination of the record that the progress of the trial indicated the theory of the people to be a claim of acute poisoning, but there was some evidence introduced looking towards chronic Poisoning......Unless it is so kept within bounds, and closely scanned and weighed by a jury, there is the greatest danger of a perversion of justice. We do not feel called upon to notice the other assignments of error as in a general way, we have discussed the principal points *argued before us. It follows from what has been said that the verdict and judgment against the respondent must be vacated and set aside, and a new trial granted. She will be remanded to the custody of the sheriff of Berrien County until bail is obtained, which will be granted by the circuitry court of said county in the sum of $3,000. Sherwood, C.J., concurs. Long and Champlain, JJ., concur in the result. Campbell, J. Did not sit.*

Other Books by the Author:

The Farmhouse: Mystery in the Mirror

Blood Trial - to be released October 2019

*You can check out information about these two books on my website: **tammywalls.com***

Made in the USA
Monee, IL
25 March 2020

23940767R00118